Always

in

Love

with

Lily

AUJOERAS PUBLISHING

Always
in
Love
with
Lily

Cathryn K. Thompson

Always in Love with Lily is a work of fiction. Names, characters, places, and incidents are products of the author's imagination or are used fictitiously. Any resemblance to actual events, locales, or persons, living or dead, is entirely coincidental.

Cover design: Fulcrum Creatives
Cover images: Getty Images

For Joseph and Audrey

Thank you for your patience and for the hours of mom time you gave up to help me make this dream come true.

With many thanks to Tara who's read all of my drafts, to Debby Cooper for her extensive feedback, to Dani Hall at DMH Editing for fixing my issues, and to Glenna, Rose, and Eric for their advice and support. Special thanks to Lynn, my constant sounding board and biggest cheerleader.

PROLOGUE

Lily stared out the small window through the blinds at the mountains in the distance. The bright blue skies of a cool Montana afternoon were giving way to the orange and pink hues of a beautiful sunset. Tony would love this view, she thought. He was always partial to sunsets. From their first kiss to long walks and dinners for two, sunsets were always a part of the equation. The perfect backdrop to any romantic scene. She wished with every fiber of her being that he were there to share this one with her.

She dropped her gaze to the parking lot below. A young girl in a sports uniform moved slowly as she attempted to get the hang of a pair of crutches. A woman, presumably her mother, hovered at her side carrying a purple leopard-patterned backpack. The woman's arms immediately reached out each time the girl faltered, but retracted just as quickly as the girl stopped short and stared. An elderly gentleman in a windbreaker and a checked cap pushed a woman in a wheelchair toward their car. They paused a moment near a young couple carrying an infant car seat and peered at the tiny newborn bundle tucked into the seat. Lily smiled and wiped a tear from her cheek.

Muffled sounds from the hallway slowly drew her attention away from the window. Nurses chatted and speakers paged doctors with urgent business, but despite the hustle and bustle outside, the room was too quiet. Over the past several weeks she'd grown so used to the beeping of monitors and the hiss of the blood pressure cuff as it completed its hourly check that the silence was uncomfortable.

Lily took a cleansing breath, trying to suppress the wave of nausea and disbelief that washed over her. She sat on the edge of the empty bed and skimmed her hand over the crisp white sheet.

There was a gentle knock before the door creaked open. "Ms. Josephson?"

Lily turned to see a jovial-looking nurse in mauve-colored scrubs peeking in on her.

"Are you doing okay?"

"Yes, thanks," Lily nodded. "I'll be fine."

"Is there anything that you need?"

"Can you get me Tony?" Lily said, her voice rising in a skeptical tone.

"I wish I could." The nurse shook her head and smiled sympathetically. "How about a cold bottle of water or something to eat?"

"No. Really. I'll be on my way in a bit. As soon as my brother gets here."

"Okay. If you think of anything..."

"Thank you, Wanda," Lily said, squinting to see the name on her tag.

Wanda nodded and stepped out, pulling the door closed behind her.

Lily stood again and began to pace, hands on her hips, then stopped and threw her head back with a groan. "Oh, Tony," she said, staring upward, "I still can't believe it. How is it even possible?"

The door opened again and Danny stepped in. "You know what they say? If you start to answer yourself—"

"Oh! Smart ass!" Lily snapped at him, but her eyes shone with love. She rushed to Danny and threw her arms around him, tears suddenly streaming down her face.

"Hey, Sissy," he whispered soothingly.

"I'm so glad you're here."

"I'm sorry I couldn't get here sooner. Are you all right? We were so worried about you."

"I will be." She wiped her cheeks with her sleeve, chuckling to draw attention away from her outburst.

"What happened?"

"Not here. Please. I just want to get out of here."

"Right," Danny nodded. "Do you have everything? Do you have a jacket or something? It's a bit nippy out there."

Lily picked up Tony's football sweatshirt and slipped it over her head. It still smelled faintly of him, which made her smile and ache for him all at once. She picked up her purse and paused to take one last glance out the

3

window at the beautiful landscape beyond the city. She looked down once more at the lot. The people she had studied just moments before were gone, replaced by new couples and families preparing to make their journeys home.

"Are you sure you're ready?" Danny said.

Truthfully, she wasn't sure. Was she really ready to leave the past—leave *him*—behind? Could she put all of the pain behind her and start over? What would become of her— personally or professionally? Life as she knew it was over. She would never be the same. Still, she knew she had to move forward, to start fresh and face the unknown.

"Lil?" Danny said to get her attention.

Lily nodded. She looked around the room one more time—grabbed her half-full bottle of water from the bedside table.

"Come on, then," Danny said. He put his arm around her and ushered her out the door.

Six weeks earlier....

1
NOT JUST ANOTHER MONDAY

The irritating screech of the alarm woke Tony from a troubled sleep. He'd jolted himself awake several times in the night with one disturbing dream after another. He turned over, hoping to find Lily, but was met by nothing more than cold sheets and an empty pillow.

He dragged himself out of bed and into the expansive master bath, thinking that he would feel better after a good, hot shower. A quick look in the mirror as he waited for the water to heat up reminded him that he was not, in fact, as old and tired as he felt. Sure, there were a few grays peppering his sandy blond hair, but his muscular physique went a long way to compensate for them. He exhaled forcefully, then with a half-smile and a tilt of his head he said, "Chin up." He stepped out of his pajama pants and into the shower, allowing the near-scalding water to wash the fog away.

Once dressed, Tony headed downstairs. He found Lily in a seated twist on a yoga mat in the middle of their loft-like living room.

"Good morning, angel," he said, stopping on the last step.

"Oh! Hey! Morning, love," Lily answered. She unfolded herself and reconstructed the pose, facing him with a bright smile.

He couldn't help but stare at her and smile back. Even in workout clothes at the crack of dawn with her hair thrown up in a messy ponytail, she was the most beautiful woman he'd ever seen. He shook his head in amazement.

"What's that for?" she asked.

"You," he said.

She cut the stretch short and rose to meet him. "Why?" she said, dabbing at the back of her neck with her towel.

He stepped down and approached. "Because you're incredibly sexy, even when you're all twisted up like a Bavarian pretzel."

"Hmm. Giving you ideas, am I?" She gave him a rather lengthy kiss.

"A few," he said, smacking his lips in response to the salty taste of hers. "You taste a bit like a pretzel too," he teased.

"Ha! Sorry. I'm a bit of a mess."

"A hot mess," he said with a wink and a purr in his voice.

"Did you sleep well?" she said. She walked toward the kitchen.

Tony followed. "I might have done. If you'd been in bed next to me," he said, with a slightly pouty face.

She looked over her shoulder and stuck her bottom lip out playfully as she crossed the room. "I'm sorry," she said again. "By the time I was ready for bed it was so late that I didn't want to wake you, so I just camped out on the sofa."

"Hmm. What did he want?"

"Charles? Only to rehash the Director's Guild Awards for the fourth time since Saturday," she said. "And the PGAs from last month. Coffee?"

"Please," he said, taking a seat on one of the stools at the large island. "Didn't he win?"

"Producer's Guild, yes, but not the Director's Guild. Now he'll fret until after the Academy Awards." She filled two mugs and handed one to him.

"Great," Tony said.

"What?" Lily said.

She noted the sour look on his face. "Are you bothered?"

"Bothered? By what? The fact that you didn't come to bed last night because you were too busy FaceTiming all of your L.A. friends and chatting to your ex-husband?"

"Yes. That." She moved around the counter and stood next to his stool.

He turned to face her. "Should I be bothered?"

"No. Because you—" She stepped between his legs and took his face in her hands. "—have absolutely nothing to worry about."

"I could use a bit more reassuring," he teased.

She set her cup down, took his cup from his hand, and set it on the counter next to him. "With pleasure," she said. She wrapped her arms around him and kissed him again, passionately. Relentlessly.

Good God, what she did to him. Any worries he'd had since waking up were temporarily forgotten. Instinctively, one hand slipped under her tank top and skimmed across her bare back. The other slid down to take hold of her firm buttocks.

She grabbed onto the lapels of his sport coat, threatening to remove it. Only then did he pull away.

"No," he whispered.

"No?" she said, brows raised.

"No. I can't, darling. I need to get going." He made an attempt to get up, but she wasn't budging.

"It's still early."

"I know. But I have an... a meeting on my way to the office, and you know how Manhattan traffic is." He had no intention of telling her where he was going. No need to worry her unnecessarily.

"It's seven a.m. What sort of person meets their architect at seven a.m.?" she asked. She continued her advances, kissing him behind the ear.

"Ah...," he moaned in response to her teeth on his earlobe. "Not that kind of meeting. Not a client. Just an... an appointment." It took everything he had to resist her as she worked her way down his jaw line. "Aw, Lil, please," he said. With his hands on her hips, he gave her a gentle shove and stood up before she could start in again. "I'm sorry sweetheart, but I really need to go."

"What about breakfast?"

"I haven't got time, love." He checked his briefcase for all necessary items before picking it up off of the dining table.

Lily took his overcoat out of the closet and held it out for him to put on.

"Thank you," he said.

"Dinner in tonight?"

"Sure."

"With any luck, we can celebrate!" she grinned.

She was talking about her latest audition, but he was hoping to have other reasons to celebrate. He gave her his most charismatic smile.

"Have a nice day," she said. She touched his cheek lovingly.

"I'll do my best," he said. He tilted her chin up with two fingers to give her one last gentle kiss. "I love you," he said, and he was out the door.

"I love you more," she called after him.

He didn't have to look back to know she was smiling when she said it, but he did, just to catch one more glimpse of her. That smile still amazed him. It saw him off, welcomed him home, lifted his spirits, and calmed his nerves. He could see that smile when he closed his eyes. He could actually hear it when she spoke his name. For years, he'd only imagined what it would be like to see that smile again, to know that it was meant for him. That smile was everything. *She* was everything. He could only hope life wouldn't be so cruel as to tear them apart after such a short time. Not after it had taken them so long to find their way back to each other.

"Dear God," he whispered as he stepped into the elevator.

As the car jolted and began its descent to Fifth Avenue, he reminded himself not to be concerned with the Charles situation. After all, Charles wasn't his only problem at the moment.

2
NO LUCK

Tony tossed his keys down on the kitchen counter. He could smell dinner cooking in the oven. "Lily...," he called out to her. "Where are you, darling?" No answer.

He strode through the room to the windows, taking in the view of Fifth Avenue and Central Park. After a minute, something caught his eye. Lily. She was still some ways off, down the block, coming out of the park across the street, but he'd know her silhouette, the way she moved, anywhere.

He watched her float up the avenue, the February breeze blowing her long dark hair. She was pushing Jocelyn, a little bundle of delight in her tiny, pale blue pea coat. As they waited for the light to change, Lily peered around the stroller and Jocelyn reached up to grab at Lily's hair. He imagined Lily, the doting aunt, cooing at the little girl in a happy, high-pitched voice about the birds, or the trees, or jokingly giving her fashion tips for the future. He smiled at the thought. It was the first time he'd smiled since he'd left her that morning. But seeing Lily with Jocelyn always brought mixed emotions.

Tony knew Lily cherished every moment with Jocelyn, so much so that she refused to entertain the notion of moving back to London permanently. But spending time with Jocelyn was bittersweet for Lily, too. At the end of the day, she always had to give her back to her parents and send her home.

Tony knew Lily wanted more than anything to have a child of her own—a child of *their* own. They'd talked about trying one day. Technically, they were never really trying not to. But the doctor had already told Lily that she was nearing the end of her child-bearing years, and the chances of her getting pregnant now, let alone avoiding another miscarriage, were slim to none. She cried herself to sleep the night she heard that. Tony's heart broke for her. She hid her disappointment well, the way she did any painful emotions, but it was there, beneath her calm, closed-lipped smile. He could read it in her eyes.

Those eyes—it was so easy to get lost in those expressive eyes. They were deep, chestnut pools of love and devotion, fiery orbs of passion, and, when she was angry, daggers that could pierce a man's heart. They were like windows to her very soul, and maybe his, too. He could look into them and see his entire life looking back at him.

When he heard a key turning in the lock, he returned from his reverie. In a blast of chatter and giggles, Lily and Jocelyn came backing through the door. He hurried to help them in.

"Hello, gorgeous," he said, pulling the door open wider to accommodate the stroller.

"Oh, hello, love! You startled me!" She turned her head and kissed him. "I didn't expect you home so soon," she said, lifting the little girl from the stroller and resting her on her hip to remove her coat. "How was your day?" She walked to the center of the room, scooped a blanket off the sofa and tossed it on the floor.

"It was... a day," he sighed. He followed her and helped situate the blanket and scatter a few toys.

"That good, huh?" Lily said.

"Mmm. Better now that I'm here with you," he said. He wrapped his arms around her from behind and kissed her neck. "What about you?"

"Oh, we had a lovely time, didn't we, Josie?"

"Any news? About the audition, I mean?"

"Not yet," she said.

Tony detected the irritation in her voice, but Lily kept smiling anyway. She tickled Jocelyn until the little girl was squealing with laughter. Jocelyn sat on the blanket cooing happily until she lost her balance and dumped over backward, then made a startled face and pretended to cry. When she got no sympathy from her admirers, she rolled over and grabbed for her purple puppy, giggling again when the checkered ears made a crinkly sound between her fingers.

"You should have seen her today," Lily said. "I was helping her stand, you know, to work her little legs, and she was moving them so quickly, stomping about, she was practically dancing."

"Really?"

"Yes! I think she's going to be a natural. I can't wait to get her into a pair of dance shoes."

"You might let her learn to walk first," Tony said with a chuckle.

"I know that, silly! It's just exciting. That's all."

Tony stood and scooped up the baby. "Don't worry, sweetheart! Your daddies and I won't let your Auntie Lily get carried away!" Jocelyn laughed again as he swung her around.

"You are so good with her," Lily said, standing. "She absolutely adores you. Come to think of it, so do I," she smiled.

"The feeling is mutual. On both counts," he said. He leaned in to kiss her again.

"I'd better check on dinner. Can you keep an eye on her? Danny and Steven should be here any minute to pick her up."

He and followed her into the kitchen with Jocelyn. "Are they staying for dinner?" he asked.

"Nope. I thought we'd have a nice quiet dinner tonight, just the two of us."

"Oh, that's good."

"Is it?"

"Yes."

"Can't wait to get your hands on me again?" she laughed.

"No... Yes... I mean, it's just nice to have an evening alone together. You've been so busy, what with the show ending and preparing for auditions. And Jocelyn."

Lily was momentarily distracted by an incoming text from her agent. "Hmm," she grunted as she fired off a quick response. She set the phone down on the island and set about preparing her green beans. "Well, I may have a lot more time for you if the next one doesn't go any better."

Tony glanced down at the messages on her screen.

"Agnes," she said, as if she sensed him looking at them.

"I'm sorry," he said.

"Eee!" Jocelyn squealed, patting his face.

"Yes, hello, darling," Tony said. He kissed her on the cheek, then turned back to Lily. "So, Thursday it is, then?"

She sighed. "I guess so."

"Does it make you nervous, auditioning?"

"No. Not exactly. I mean, I feel ready. I've been over the routines a million times. But, I have a lot to prove, don't I? I'm not twenty anymore. Let's face it. I may be running out of options."

"Don't say that," Tony said. He took Lily's hand and gave it a gentle squeeze.

"Na!" Jocelyn cried, grabbing at Tony's nose."

"Oh!" Tony traded Lily's hand for Jocelyn's and kissed her tiny fingers. "Yes, that is my nose. Let's leave it where it is, shall we?" He tapped her nose with the tip of his finger.

She giggled.

Lily watched the two of them, smiling slightly. "I love watching you with her," she whispered, then turned away quickly and cleared her throat.

He pretended not to know what that meant.

"Oh, that's turned out nice," she said, bending to pull her roast her roast from the oven. She consulted the thermometer sticking out of the center. "Hmm. Not quite."

Just then, her phone vibrated on the counter.

"Bloody hell! It's Charles," Tony said, glancing at the display.

"Ignore it. I'll call him back later," Lily said. "How was your meeting this morning?"

"What does he want now?"

"He probably wants to go for round five."

"What?"

"A full scale attack on the Director's Guild, you know. Either that or he wants me to look at his opening sequence again."

"Doesn't he have a girlfriend to complain to?"

"Ha! Yes. But not one who knows what it's like to lose an Oscar."

17

Tony continued. "For that matter, why the hell doesn't he just hire another choreographer?"

"He has. He just uses me as a consultant."

"What on earth for?"

"Thank you!"

"That's not what I meant. I know you're talented, but to keep you on as a consultant from the other side of the country—there's just something funny about it."

"Don't be silly."

"What? Don't you think it's odd?"

"Odd? If you mean the fact that he's still speaking to me, yes. I wouldn't have figured him for the amicable-divorce type. But odd that he would seek my professional opinion, no. We worked together for more than twelve years. He trusts my work. It's only natural to want the opinion of someone you trust."

"And you do hate to burn bridges, don't you?"

"I suppose I do." She shrugged. "I don't know if I can afford to cut ties with him at this point in my career. If I ever want to work again."

"Stop!"

"Well? I'm just saying." She placed the roaster back into the oven. "Anyway, it's not as if I don't get anything out of it. I have been compensated for my time. Quite well, as a matter of fact."

"Maybe. But with him—it's like he just does it to keep some kind of hold on you."

"Darling," she said, putting her potholders down on the counter and approaching him. She took the baby from him and set her in her high chair. She handed her a set of stacking cups, then turned back to him. "If anyone has a hold on me at this point, it's you." Her arms encircled his neck and she kissed the corner of his mouth ever so gently. Unlike this morning, his arms remained at his sides. His lips were unresponsive. She pulled back and regarded him curiously. "Is that all that's bothering you?"

He sighed. "I don't know."

"Surely you know how happy you make me, don't you? You know how much I love you."

"It's not you I'm worried about."

"Don't—"

"It's not as if he didn't succeed in tearing us apart once before. Unscrupulous bastard."

"Tony!"

"Well! Not to mention he jerked you around for months before filing for the divorce. What did he think—that you would change your mind?"

"Listen, I don't care what he thinks or what he does," Lily said. "He and I are friends. We still care about each other. We support each other professionally. But nothing is ever going to take you away from me again, okay? I promise."

Tony nodded, but looked away.

She took his face in her hands and kissed him again, hoping to remove any last shred of

19

doubt, then backed away, licking her lips. "Better?" she asked with a smile.

"A little," he nodded.

"Oh, that'll be Danny," Lily said when she heard the buzzer. "Come on Little Miss," she said. She picked Jocelyn up again. "Give your Uncle Tony a kiss." She held her out to him.

"Good night, sweetheart," Tony said, giving Jocelyn another peck on the cheek.

Moments later, Lily's brother burst through the door in his usual uninhibited fashion, greeting both Lily and Jocelyn with a flurry of hugs and kisses. "Cheers, mate!" he shouted to Tony as Lily ushered him into the living room and launched into a detailed report of the day.

Before Tony had a chance to join them, his mobile rang and he disappeared upstairs.

Lily was finishing up the dressing for the salad when he came shuffling back down grumbling into the phone. "I couldn't give a rat's ass right now, Sam. Just deal with it, will you? Fine. Thank you." He hit end without saying goodbye and slipped the phone into his pocket.

Surprised by his tone, Lily looked up from her emulsion. "Good Lord, what's the matter?" she asked, concerned. He was rarely that curt with anyone, let alone one of his most valuable employees.

"I told you. It's been a shit day, that's all. Has Danny gone?"

"Yes. What happened?"

"It's... nothing, all right? I'd rather not talk about it."

"You were pretty harsh with Sam just now for it to be nothing," she said nonchalantly as she continued plating the dinner salads.

"For God's sake, Lily. I just told you I don't want to talk about it!" He slumped down into one of the chairs at the kitchen table.

She eyed him for a moment, then calmly said, "Okay. Well, how do you feel about getting a bottle of wine?"

He sighed heavily as he slowly pushed himself to his feet and left the kitchen without a word. Lily could hear clanking sounds coming from the bar in the other room.

He brought a bottle of pinot noir and two glasses to the dining table.

"Good choice," she said as she met him there with the salads.

Tony set the bottle on the table and fixed his attention on uncorking it.

Lily returned to the kitchen for her basket of homemade bread. She carried it to the table, avoiding eye contact. When she tried to return to the kitchen a second time, Tony grabbed her wrist.

She turned back to face him.

"I'm sorry," he said, handing her a glass of wine. "I didn't mean to snap at you."

She shrugged it off. "You had a rough day. I didn't mean to push."

"I know you didn't."

"I just want you to know that I'm here for you if you need me."

He stared at her for a moment as if he had something to say. Instead, he took the glass back out of her hand and set them both on the table. "I always need you."

"Tony, you know what I—"

"In fact, right now," he interrupted, "I need you more than ever." He drew her into his embrace. "You have no idea." He kissed her hard and felt that familiar surge of energy.

Lily tried to answer. "I—"

Tony persisted. "I need you in the worst way." He kissed her again. "I need you in every... possible... way," he whispered, his lips now traveling the length of her neck. He spent a few extra seconds where her neck met her shoulder, knowing it was a sweet spot. Her muscles tensed, but her knees softened. He tightened his grip to steady her.

"Mmm. Tony," she murmured.

"I want you," he whispered. "I want to make love to you."

"Now?"

"Right now." His lips continued their tour, finding their way down her throat.

"What about... my roast?"

"What about it?"

"It needs to... come out of the oven in a few... It'll dry out."

"Then we'll wash it down with copious amounts of wine and make love all over again."

"I..."

22

"Lily, I *need* to be with you." There was sort of desperate quality in his voice. He kissed her one last time. It was a kiss filled with hunger and a sort of primal need that she couldn't ignore.

"Let's go, then," she said. She made a move toward the stairs, but he pulled her back again.

He bent down and lifted her up with one arm under her behind and the other supporting her back and carried her into the kitchen, assaulting her décolletage with his lips as he walked. He laid her across the large marble island and had his way with her, but not before making sure that she'd also had hers.

As Tony had suggested, their romantic interlude was followed by the bottle of pinot noir and a slightly dry pork roast, and then a bottle of Beaujolais and another interlude.

That night, Lily rested peacefully in Tony's arms while Tony drifted in and out of a fitful sleep. Around midnight he gave up trying to sleep. He kissed Lily on the head, slid out of bed, and donned a pair of pajamas, careful not to disturb her.

Two hours and a quarter of a bottle of Macallan later, Lily discovered him in his office at his desk, laptop open, staring up at the ceiling.

"Hey, you," she said.

He looked up to see her standing in the doorway in his robe with her hands in the pockets, her mussed raven hair framing her face. "Hey yourself," he said, closing the laptop and taking another swig of scotch. He watched her, mesmerized. Hands still in her pockets, she moved slowly toward him, nibbling her lower lip.

"What's up?" she asked as she inserted herself between him and the desk.

"I'll give you three guesses," he snickered, tugging at the ties on her belt until she was forced to climb onto his lap to keep from falling over. As she straddled him, he ran his hands under the velour fabric of the robe and caressed her muscular thighs. "You're not wearing anything underneath," he noted.

"Of course I'm not," she giggled. "I just threw this on when I woke up and discovered you were missing."

"Mmm. Sorry." He kissed her shoulder, now exposed, the oversized garment falling from it.

"Is that all you think about, really?" she teased.

"No. But thinking about fucking you is so much more pleasant than the other things on my mind."

"Excuse me?"

"You heard me. Let's do it again."

"All right. That's it." She leaned away, though she didn't stand up, knowing he was more vulnerable to her in their current position.

He continued trying to kiss her.

"No! Stop. Darling...," She took his face in her hands. "Come on, now. What's going on?"

"Nothing." He shook his head. "I'm busy, that's all. We're in the middle of a huge project and I can't afford to fuck it up."

"Something's happened," she said.

"No," he answered, though he realized it wasn't really a question. "It's nothing, I told you."

"Don't tell me it's nothing. I know better. You were downright rude to Sam earlier. You were snippy with me, and you chalked it up to a bad day. Now, it's two in the morning and you're sat here gettin' pissed. I don't care about that so much, but never, in all of the time we've been together, 'ave you ever referred to us *fuckin'*."

"Darling, I don't need you getting worked up."

"I'm not."

"Yes you are. You're dropping letters all over the place."

Her working-class accent was something she'd learned to control, but it had a way of sneaking out if she was too upset or excited to think about it.

She took a deep breath before speaking again. "Something is wrong and I'm not moving until you tell me what it is."

"I don't want you to move," he assured her with one last attempt at humor.

"Tony, talk to me, damn it!"

He stared at her in silence.

"Please."

"Okay," he mouthed. He moved her hands from his face to his lap, rubbing the backs of them with his thumbs. "But you have to promise me you're not going to worry."

She nodded in agreement, but she could feel her heart start to beat faster.

"I didn't want to tell you until after your audition."

"Tell me what?"

His lips turned up in a gentle smile, but it was forced. He looked away and swallowed.

"Tony?" she said, trying not to sound alarmed.

He cleared his throat, took a breath, and uttered the words that damn near stopped her racing heart.

3
NOW WHAT?

It was several moments before Lily could move. When the words finally stopped echoing in her head, she silently picked up the bottle of scotch Tony had been working on and refilled his glass. Instead of handing it to him, she took a large gulp, threw back her head, and swallowed. She stared into the glass, swirling the remaining liquid gently, willing herself to hold it together.

"What's the prognosis?" she asked, her eyes still trained on the scotch.

"I don't know yet. The results of the scans from this morning show some sort of undesirable mass in my right kidney."

"Undesirable mass? Cancer?"

"We don't know that for sure. It could be a cyst."

"But it could be cancer."

He didn't answer.

"Tony?"

"Yes. All right? It could be cancer."

She stood and began to pace, drink still in hand.

"Lily," he called out to her.

She turned away and took another drink to avoid looking at him. A moment later, she felt his hands on her shoulders.

"Lily," he whispered, "It's going to be fine."

"You don't know that."

"Darling, look at me."

She rolled her eyes and pivoted to face him, putting on a brave face.

"Do I look sick to you?"

She shook her head.

"Especially considering the workout you put me through earlier? Come on. I'm gonna be fine. Whatever it is, all right?"

She nodded. "So, what do we do now? Have you called your mother?"

"God, no! I didn't even like to tell you, let alone her."

"She would want to know."

"I'm sure she would, but there's no sense in alarming her before we have anything concrete. You know how she is." He thought for a moment and then spoke again, shaking his head vigorously. "No. No. What we do is we just... carry on. You have your audition and I fly to London to meet with Sam and the rest of the team about the plans for the performing arts center."

"Are you still planning to leave tomorrow?"

"Yes."

"So, we just ignore it for two weeks until you get back?

"I wish that were an option, but no. I'll be back Thursday night."

28

"That hardly seems worth the trip."

He shrugged. "Well, I need to be *there* for the meeting with the foundation on Wednesday, and I need to be *here* for the biopsy on Friday morning, so..."

"Christ," she said and gulped down the last swallow of scotch.

4
WAITING GAME

For the next four days Lily did as Tony
suggested. She carried on. She went to her
audition and did just about anything she
could think of to keep herself busy. On Friday
morning, she sat in the waiting room at New
York Presbyterian, feeling tense and uneasy.
The procedure was supposed to take less than
an hour. But an hour and fifteen minutes
went by without a word from the nurse at the
desk and Lily was becoming restless. Every
second felt like an eternity. The thoughts
she'd fought so hard to keep at bay for the
past few days were gnawing at her. Left alone
with her thoughts, she drifted into a dark
place.

Cancer, she thought. The word
reverberated in her head and sent a chill
through her body. Why? She knew better than
to ask, really. It didn't matter that he was the
healthiest, fittest, most virile man she knew.
Cancer didn't discriminate. Still, she couldn't
help but think about the unfairness of it all.
After so many years, they were finally

together, and now this. It galled her to think of all the precious time they'd wasted.

What might have happened if she'd never left New York all those years ago? What if she had secured a spot in the Royal Ballet? What if she hadn't let Tony go so easily? What if she'd never married Charles? There would never be any answers to those questions, and it didn't do any good to think about what might have been.

She fished in her handbag for her phone. A kind word or a joke from her brother would go a long way right now. She pulled up her favorites list, but stopped before selecting Danny's name. As much as she needed to talk to someone, she'd promised Tony it would be their secret until they had more information. It made her crazy to agree to such a thing. She was sure his family would want to know. But, she also knew that he hated to have people hovering over him fretting, and once his mother and sister knew, they were bound to surround him like she-bears. Tony didn't need that—and neither did Lily.

She put the phone in her lap and stared at the local news on the waiting room television. The sound was muted, and being forced to read the closed captions provided a brief distraction. When she tired of reading the sports results, she stood and stretched. She paced for a while then sat back down. When she looked at the television again, Shawna Spencer was giving her entertainment news report. Lily picked up her phone again and stared at Charles's name, which was still in her favorites list despite the fact that the divorce had been finalized more than a month ago. For a moment Lily wondered if it was inappropriate to call her ex-husband while waiting for her lover to get out of surgery.

Lover. It made her relationship with Tony sound tawdry. *Boyfriend* made it sound childish. What word could possibly describe her relationship with Tony?

She shook her head, irritated by her own wandering mind and considered calling Charles again. It would give her something to think about. She didn't have to tell him anything about Tony. And even if she let it slip, what harm could it do? He was close enough to her to care, but far enough removed that he wouldn't bother Tony. She swallowed hard, exhaled, and dialed.

"Hello?"

"Hello, Charles. It's me... ah... Lily."

"Yes. I know. This is a surprise," he said.

"Yes. How are you?"

"Fine. You?"

"Good," she lied. She glanced at her watch and realized that, in her desperation, she'd forgotten to consider the time difference. "Oh. I'm sorry. It's early, isn't it?"

"It's okay. We were actually already in the office."

"Oh. Well, if you're busy—"

"No, Lil. It's fine. We can take a break."

"Ah, okay."

"So?"

"Well, you called the other day and I finally had a moment to call you back, so..."

"I'm glad you did," he said.

"So, was there something you wanted?"

"Not really. I thought you'd want to know that we used your suggestions for the party scene."

"That's great."

"Yes. It is great. Editing is just about finished."

"I'm glad I could be of help."

"I never doubted it."

"Good. That's good."

"And," Charles continued, "I have some news that I thought you might be interested in."

"What's that?"

"I've heard rumors of a *Last Dance* reunion special."

"No!"

"Yes!"

"I didn't think they'd ever do that after the sequel fiasco."

"Like I said—rumors. But tell Agnes to keep her ears open. If it's true, you should hear something soon."

"I will."

"And... I had dinner with Robert Mitchell the other night."

"Yes."

"He told me that he's planning a Christmas special for this year and it just so happens he needs a choreographer."

"Really? I thought he was dating that choreographer. What's her name?"

"Megan Shaw."

"Right."

"He was. Past tense."

"They broke up?"

"Yes. I thought you might be interested."

"I'd love to," she said. She had always wanted to do a Christmas special. "But I do have a lot of things going on right now."

"Like what?"

"Well, for one thing, I had an audition with Justine Sorenson yesterday, and I was... you know I'm... still waiting to hear."

"Oh. How did it go?" Charles said, seeming genuinely interested.

"It went well, I think."

"Do you think you'll get it?"

"I don't know. I hope so."

"Are you okay?"

"What? I'm fine. Why wouldn't I be?"

"You sound strange."

Lily quickly changed the subject. "What about you? How are you? How's the hip doing?"

"Oh... well, like I told you, I'm a better predictor of rain than the local weather authorities," he chuckled. "But other than that it doesn't give me much trouble anymore.

"How's Cora? Everything okay with the two of you?"

"Cora's great. She's generally always great, you know?"

"Yes. She is. You should really hold on to her, you know? She's a good woman. A little young for you maybe, but a good woman. Even if she did steal you away." She let out a small hint of laughter.

"Ha! She's only four years younger that you and she didn't steal me. You left me, remember?"

"Hmm. Okay, you win. So... listen... I guess I'd better go."

"Already?"

"Yeah. Yes. I should probably..."

He heard her let out a painful sigh on the other end of the phone. "Lillian? What's wrong?"

She avoided the issue, knowing full well that Tony would consider it some kind of betrayal if she told Charles, no matter how hard she tried to justify it. She should never have called him.

"Lil?"

"I should follow up with Justine, you know, and—" She was interrupted by the brush of a hand on her arm. "Ah... just a minute, Charles." She looked up at the nurse standing beside her chair.

"It took longer than expected for the sedatives to kick in, but the procedure is finished," she said. "Mr. Ward is on his way to recovery now. You can see him in a few minutes."

"Thank you. Did the doctor say anything?" Lily said without thinking.

"He'll be in to talk to you both," the nurse said.

"Doctor?" Charles said on the other end of the line. "Lil, what's going on?"

"Charles, thanks for calling," Lily said, flustered. In ten years of marriage he'd barely heard a word she'd said. Leave it to him to pick this exact moment to start listening.

"You called me," Charles pointed out.

"What? Oh, so I did." Lily hurriedly said goodbye and hung up before he could say anything else. She pulled her compact from her bag and checked her make-up. Silly as it was, she wanted to look her best when Tony saw her again. She couldn't have him thinking she'd spent the whole morning crying. She had just finished touching up her eyes when the nurse returned to escort her to Tony's room. She whispered a quick prayer of thanks and gathered up her belongings.

Tony was still groggy from the sedatives when they let Lily back to see him. "Hey, baby!" he said when he saw her.

"Oh, now I know you must still be under the influence of the drugs," she said, smiling at him, "'cause you of all people know better than to call me that!"

"Sorry. I think I am a little out of it. Hot stuff!"

"You are incorrigible!" She leaned in and kissed him. He placed a hand firmly on her behind. She jumped. "Ooh! Good Lord, Tony!" She sat on the edge of the bed and held his hand. "I guess I don't need to ask you how you're feeling."

"How I'm feeling depends on what exactly they found in there."

"I don't think they know yet. They'll get back to us as soon as they know something."

"Within the week," he sighed.

"Within the week," she echoed.

"Hmm. Do you have my phone on you?"

"What for?"

"I want to call Sam and see how his meeting went this morning."

"Already? Can't it wait?"

"It can, but I don't want it to."

"I doubt you're even supposed to use your phone in here," she said, fishing it out of her purse.

"I'll take my chances." He clicked the on button but got nothing. "Damn! My battery's gone. I must have forgotten to charge it last night while my gorgeous girlfriend was distracting me."

"While *I* was distracting *you*?"

"Yes. Can I have yours, please?" He held out his hand.

"You do have a selective memory, don't you? Fine. But I wish you'd take it easy for five minutes." She handed the phone to him. He hit the button and read the notifications on the lock screen.

"You've got a text from Charles. Again."

- **You still haven't answered my question. Call me.**

"What's that about?" he asked.

"Nothing. We can talk about it later."

"I want to talk about it now."

"Darling, calm down. Please."

"I don't want to calm down. What question? Coming up with a back-up plan, are you? In case I don't make it? Picking up where you left off?" He glared at her.

She stared back, silent at first, her lips pursed. "Anthony Francis Ward, you know that's not true." She paused, looking into his eyes, head tipped to one side. She gently caressed his cheek. "You're scared. I get that. Whether or not you'll admit it. But I'm not going to let you do this. I'm not going to let you lash out at me. We're in this together. We need to stick together. Not fall apart. I only called him because... well, I couldn't stand just sitting there anymore."

Tony was quiet for a moment. This situation was just as stressful for her as it was for him. He shook his head. "I'm sorry," he said.

"I know."

He raised her hand to his lips and kissed it. "Forgive me."

She smiled at him as if to say there was no need. "And if you must know," she said, "he wanted to tell me about a project that Robert Mitchell is working on. A Christmas special."

"Oh?"

"Robert may need a choreographer."

"What did you tell him?"

"I told him I had a few other things to worry about right now."

"I don't want you worrying about me. I told you that."

"Yes, you did. But I worry anyway. Besides, I'm still waiting to hear about the show."

"Any news?"

She shook her head. "Looks like all we can do is wait."

"It's so frustrating," he said.

"I know," she said, fully aware that neither one of them was really talking about the show.

5
WAKE UP CALL

Lily crept into their bedroom late Monday morning after her workout. Tony was still sleeping peacefully. She put his mug of hot coffee and her phone down on the bedside table and sat on the edge of bed next to him. She watched him for a few minutes, and caught herself wondering how many more of these mornings they would get. Then she shook it off with a quiet sigh and reached out to touch his cheek.

A smile softened his strong face. "Morning, angel," he said, his eyes still closed.

"Good morning, sleepy head," she said. "How are you feeling?"

He paused and stretched. "Fine."

"Really? No pain or anything?"

"Lil, it's been three days. You can stop worrying."

"I know. You're right."

"I feel good. In fact, I feel better than good," he said as he wrapped a hand around the back of her neck and pulled her down to kiss him.

She indulged him, then tried to fake a smile as she handed him his coffee, but her hunched shoulders gave her away.

He inhaled the steam and the rich, nutty scent, watching her closely over the rim of the cup. "What's wrong?" he said. He took a sip.

"I texted Justine this morning, you know, just to check in."

"And?"

"I didn't get it."

"You're kidding!"

She picked up her phone, pulled up the text, and showed him the screen.

- **Hi Justine. Just wanted to say thanks for the opportunity. It was great to see you. Take care.**

- It was great to see you too, Lily. So sorry things are not going to work out. Best, Justine.

"That's it? No other indication as to why?"

She shook her head again. "I know why." She stood and walked toward the master bath, peeling off her tank top as she went. "I'm old," she said as she turned on the shower.

"What?"

"I'm old," she said again from the doorway as she waited for the water to heat up.

"Lily, don't be ridiculous." He had to work to stifle a laugh. "You are not old!" He took his phone off the bedside table to check for missed calls.

41

She went on. "In my business I am, Tony! You know, I talked to Danny. He heard they hired Carrie Corothers."

"So?"

"So, she's a fabulous performer. She's got gorgeous legs and long dark hair."

"So do you!"

"And she's twenty-three."

"But you've got experience."

"Yeah, well, it would appear that they didn't want someone with quite so much *experience*," she said with finger quotations. "Face it, Tony. I'm past it."

His eyes ran over her as she stood there, arms folded over a body to die for, in nothing but yoga pants and a sports bra. He burst out laughing. He couldn't help it. The thought was ludicrous.

"Thanks a lot!" She sniffed and walked away.

"Lil..." He climbed out of bed, turned off the shower, and followed her into the walk-in closet, dropping his phone on the bench at the foot of the bed.

"Maybe I just need to face the facts," she said as she shuffled through her clothing options.

"What facts?"

"Over eighty percent of dancers are twenty-six to thirty-five."

"Statistics can be—"

"And those who try to keep going into their forties... well, it's only a matter of time before injuries begin to slow them down. Look at

Wendy Wahlen. She was forty-four when she had to stop."

"Lily…" He took the blouse out of her hand and hung it back on the rack. "Come here." He took her by the hand and pulled her toward the full-length mirror. "Tell me what you see."

She didn't answer, though "washed-up, out of work, pre-menopausal, hot mess" crossed her mind.

He watched her eyes get watery. "I'll tell you what I see. I see a beautiful, healthy, strong woman with an incredible body and more grace and style than she knows what to do with. If the world of show business can't see that, it's their loss."

Lily gave him a pouty smile in the mirror. "You're blinded by love."

"Oh, no. I see you quite clearly, my darling," he said, wrapping his arms around her from behind. "Every. Beautiful. Inch," he said, kissing his way along her long, slender neck.

"Hmm. Are sure it's not just the pain killers talking?"

"Hardly. I haven't taken a thing," he whispered, moving on to the other side of her neck. "I can feel absolutely everything."

She pivoted to face him. "Are you sure you're all right?"

"I'm fine, darling. Pain… is not the sensation I was referring to."

Seeing the look on his face made her blush. Embarrassed by her own alarmist behavior, she tried to brush it off. "You never stop, do you?" she said with a playful shove.

He staggered backward, feigning shock. "You struck me! How dare you! I'm recovering from surgery, remember?"

"Now you want to play that card?"

"I think I'd better if you're going to get violent," he laughed, bringing her into his arms.

"Then you'd better get back into bed."

"Only if you'll come with me."

"What?"

"Come on," he said, wrangling her toward the bed."

"Don't hurt yourself," she said through her giggles.

"Then don't fight me."

She didn't. She toddled along with him as he pulled her across the room, entranced by his boyish smile. She loved that smile. When they reached the bed he turned and pushed her down upon it with gentle force. He leaned over her and kissed her until she thought she might never catch her breath. She gasped once when his lips finally left her mouth and again as his hands slipped under the edge of her sports bra and thrust it up, freeing her breasts, exposing them to his eager lips.

"Tony!" she cried.

"Hmm?" he mumbled, his mouth still otherwise occupied.

"We can't. Not for at least two weeks."

He ignored her warning.

"Doctor's orders," she said between breaths. "Don't start something you can't finish."

By the time she got the words out, skillful as he was, he'd already managed to work off her yoga pants. He gripped her tiny waist with his strong hands, pinning her as he kissed his way down her abdomen. Her toned body undulated with pleasure and anticipation at the soft touch of his lips.

His thumbs traced their way over her hips and caught in the waistband of her panties. He placed a final kiss just below her belly button and looked up at her, grinning wickedly. "Just because I can't finish, doesn't mean you can't."

Unfortunately, before Tony could carry out his plans, they were interrupted by his Marimba ringtone. Distracted, he glanced at the phone. The name on the display got his attention. "Fuck!" he started.

"What's wrong?" Lily asked, pulling herself up on her elbows to look at him.

"I'm sorry, darling. I have to take this."

"What? No!" she moaned.

Before she could protest any more, Tony was walking out of the room.

She stared after him, hoping for a speedy return, cursing whomever was on the other end.

Tony returned a few minutes later. Judging by the look on his face, it was no kind of social call.

"That was Dr. Branson's office," he said as he sat heavily on the edge of the bed.

She scrambled for her discarded tank top as feelings of frustrated desire were overcome by dread. "That was quick. Did they have the results?"

He nodded.

"Good or bad?"

"I don't know yet. He wants to see me at two o'clock this afternoon."

6
STRIKE ONE

The drive home was a silent one, as Lily and Tony each waited for the other to speak. It was, overall, good news. The tumor had been removed and they had reason to believe that they got it all. But Lily still couldn't squelch the nagging feeling in the pit of her stomach. Her head pounded as the overactive, over-dramatic side of her brain attempted to overtake the calm, optimistic side. *Malignant.* She felt the knot in her stomach tighten again. That word stung even more than the "C" word itself, she thought.

Once home, she headed for the kitchen to put on a kettle for tea. Tony followed her. She stood at the stove, unable to make eye contact with him. She knew full well that if she looked into his eyes there would be no way to avoid a breakdown.

He stepped up behind her. "Lily," he said softly, putting his arms around her.

"Do you want a cup of tea?" she asked.

He ignored her question. "You were awfully quiet all the way home."

She continued to face the stove as if the kettle wouldn't function without her direct supervision.

"You are aware that we just got good news, aren't you?"

Lily nodded. "I know."

"But?" he said.

She shook her head.

Tony knew she was working out all possible scenarios. He could hear the silent "What if" in her trembling voice.

"Do you want to talk about it?"

She didn't answer.

"Avoiding it won't make it go away, you know," he said.

"I know that."

"You heard what the doctor said. They made the right choice with the open biopsy. They think they got the whole tumor."

"They also said it was an aggressive cancer and that the odds of reoccurrence were—"

"Hey..." He leaned his chin on her shoulder. "It's going to be okay."

"You're sure about that?"

"Yes."

"How?"

"I don't know. I just know that we're going get through it. I didn't wait twelve years to get you back just to let cancer take me away from you."

"Which is why you should have a second opinion." She turned toward him and buried her face in his chest.

"I didn't say I wouldn't. I'd just rather deal with it here." He could feel her shake as she took in a deep breath to stifle the tears on the horizon. "Darling," he said frowning over her shoulder, "what's got you so upset?"

He gently tipped her chin upward so he could see her face. As she'd predicted, the moment he did, the water works began.

He pulled out a handkerchief and she took it to blot her eyes.

"I'm sorry," she said shaking her head. She turned away again and took out two cups for tea. "I just wish you would at least consider Channing."

"Why?"

"Why not?"

"First of all, because I loathe California and you know that."

"But Eric Channing is one of the most respected in his field. People line up to see him, and he's offering to see you. And you heard what Dr. Branson said about him— about his research."

"I don't like that, either. The fact that this guy calls Branson out of nowhere, gets all the details to my case out of him and—"

"It wasn't out of nowhere."

"What?"

She handed him his cup with a sigh. "He called because... because I asked him to."

"Oh," Tony said.

"I called him last week to ask if he might be able to see you. He first said no, but I guess he had an opening."

Distaste still flickered in Tony's eyes. "So, you called in a favor?"

"What difference does that make? He's a damn good doctor who also happens to be a good friend," she said.

Tony shook his head. "Darling, I just don't think I need to fly across the country into my own personal hell to find a good doctor when I can see someone right here at home."

"Okay." She shrugged, defeated. "You're right. It's your choice. I just wanted the best care for you. That's all. You do whatever you need to do. Just... let me know what I can do to help."

"Would you like to be the one to call my mother?" he joked. He pulled her into a one-armed hug, careful not to spill either of their cups of tea.

"Not funny," she said. But she laughed in spite of herself.

They moved into the living room and settled on the sofa. Wrapped up in a blanket, looking out over Central Park, they drank their tea in silence.

About an hour later, Lily's phone vibrated on the end table. She picked it up and read it. Tony glanced over her shoulder and read: Dr. Eric Channing.

- **Did Branson tell you I had an opening?**

She turned off the screen without typing a response and stood reluctantly. "I'd better get started on dinner. My Coq au Vin isn't going to prepare itself, is it?"

"Lil," Tony said. He reached for her hand, preventing her from leaving. "Tell him thank you and ask him when we should be there," he said.

Her eyes questioned him.

"You trust him," he said. A realization, not a question.

She nodded. "I do. Completely," she said. "But I don't want you to do this just because you think I—"

"And Dr. Branson says he comes highly recommended. So..."

She was tempted to ask why the change of heart, but she thought it best to simply accept his decision. She smiled as she squeezed his hand. "Thank you," she said.

"One condition." He held up a finger.

"Anything."

"We don't stay in Charles's guest room!"

"Ha! I'll make sure of that!"

"Okay, then. You get started on the travel arrangements. I'll call my mother."

She bent down and kissed him on the cheek. "Good luck," she said.

He gave her a forced smile as she left the room.

7
HOLLYWOOD HOLIDAY

Ten days later they arrived in Los Angeles. The sight of palm trees rising against a sunny, blue sky would have made most people smile. Not Tony. He sighed heavily as the car pulled up in front of the Beverly Wilshire Hotel.

"What's the matter?" Lily asked.

"It's nothing. It's silly."

"What?"

"It's just…"

"Tell me."

"The last time I took you to L.A., I lost you. I know it's silly to think about that, but…"

"That's never going to happen again. I promise."

He nodded. "There's just this negative vibe for me, you know?"

"Well, think of it this way. Now we've got a chance to make new memories and some positive *vibes*," she said in a mocking tone. "Come on!"

Lily hopped out of the cab and peered at the driver over the rim of her designer sunglasses as he removed their bags from the trunk.

"Thank you, sir," he said as Tony handed him a tip.

As the car pulled away, Tony picked up Lily's bag and was shocked to find it weighed next to nothing. "No wonder you didn't need me to carry your bag down this morning," he said. "It's practically empty."

Lily laughed out loud. "I know!"

"Where are all of your clothes?"

"Tony, look around you," she said, gesturing with an open palm.

He squinted against the afternoon sun at the bright white store fronts across the way and shrugged.

"Chanel, Louis... Rodeo Drive!" she said. "Need I say more?"

He laughed and shook his head. "Don't you have things you need for tonight?"

"Oh, darling," she whispered standing so close to him that her lips were practically touching his, "I have needs, but none of them are material at the moment."

"Is that a fact?"

He leaned in to kiss her, but she backed away with a salacious smile and turned toward the hotel.

"Oh... that hurts," he laughed. "Deny me, will you?"

She just laughed as she made her way to the reception desk.

"I still can't believe you brought a near empty suitcase," he said as they waited for the elevator.

Lily looked around to be sure no one was listening.

"Tony, we haven't had sex in over two weeks. I've got a toothbrush and an extra pair of panties. I don't plan on needing anything else."

He raised his eyebrows at her.

"Once I get you into bed, I don't plan on getting out."

The elevator doors opened and she stepped in.

He followed, his heart starting to race at the thought. "Not getting out of bed? You must be exhausted, then. Hmm?"

"Oh, I'm tired all right," she said as the doors closed. "Tired of waiting!"

Before Tony knew what was happening, she dropped her bag, shoved him up against the rear wall of the elevator, threw her arms around his neck and kissed him. They didn't come up for air until the doors opened on the twelfth floor. Even then, it was only long enough to sprint to their suite.

The elegant decor throughout the period building created a lovely ambience. Their corner suite had two separate balconies with stunning views of downtown Los Angeles and Hollywood Hills, classically elegant furnishings in rich reds and browns, and a large, sunlit marble bath. But they may as well have been at a La Quinta for all the two of them cared at that moment. The room had a door with a lock and a bed and, therefore, checked all of the boxes.

Tony opened the door and paused for Lily to enter. Once inside, they both tossed their bags down and Lily launched herself into him again, throwing him against the door as she slammed it closed.

"Take it easy, tigress," he laughed, breaking free of her lip lock.

"Sorry. Did I hurt you?" she asked, already breathing heavily.

"No. All of the important parts are still intact."

"Thank God!"

They both laughed and went back for more.

"Do you have... any idea... how much... I want you... right now?" he whispered.

"Yes!"

"Yes?"

"So..."

"So?"

"Tony, just... stop talking... and take me."

She didn't have to tell him again. Their clothes fell to the floor piece by piece in a fit of frenzied passion, leaving a trail through the sitting room into the bedroom.

"See! What did I tell you? New *vibes*," Lily said, falling on to her side of the bed after the dismount.

"You're right," Tony said. He rolled over to spoon her and breathed in her ear. "This is already far better than my last trip to L.A."

"Ha! Good Lord, Tony!"

"What?"

"Was it always like this?"

"Do you mean that in a good way or a bad way?"

"In a fabulous way."

"Then, yes."

"My God, I'm completely knackered," she said. "Aren't you? I mean, you were... wild!"

"I was wild? You attacked me in the elevator."

"You liked it."

"Ha! True! Ah, well," he said, rolling onto his back. "I think maybe we were both making up for lost time. Then again, I have cancer and you're forty-four and past it," he teased. "Perhaps exhaustion is to be expected."

"Hey!"

"I'm kidding!" he said, leaning over her and kissing her again.

She playfully fought him until his kiss became so intense that she had to acquiesce.

"Oh, bloody hell!" Tony said when a knock at the door interrupted them.

"Ah ha! Perhaps those are our extra towels. I can't believe there were only two in there to begin with," Lily said. "Budget cuts!" she laughed.

"I'll get them," Tony said, sitting up.

"Oh, no. Let me." She sat up too and kissed his shoulders. "You rest."

"I can get it. I'm not incapable."

She climbed out of bed and dashed for the bathroom to grab one of the plush terry robes. "I know. You're quite capable. You've just proven that, but I'm planning on taking advantage of you again in a bit and I'd like for you to be ready!"

"Ha! Fine. I shall try to prepare myself."

She turned back and smiled at him from the doorway.

"What's that grin for?"

"You."

"Why?"

"Because you're devastatingly handsome and sexy and I absolutely adore you."

"And I you, darling," he called back.

Lily walked toward the door, tying her robe as she went. She was met with quite a surprise when she opened it.

"Charles? What the hell are you doing here?"

"Hello, Lillian," Charles said, his eyes scanning her as she stood stunned in the doorway. "How are you? Are you okay?"

"I'm fine," she said.

"Really?"

"Yes. Why?"

"Good." He pushed his way into the room without being invited.

"Charles, what is this about?"

"I heard you were here."

"You heard?"

"Yes. Word gets around in this town. You know that."

"Of course it does." She followed him into the sitting area and moved to close the door to the bedroom.

"He looked at her again and then at his watch. "It's not even seven o'clock. You weren't sleeping, were you?"

"Ah, no." She ran her hands through her hair trying to straighten it.

"Good. You know you shouldn't go to bed this early or the jetlag will kill you. Is Tony here?"

"Yes. He's—"

"Never mind," Charles said without waiting for her to finish. "You can tell him later."

"Tell him what?"

"I came to invite the two of you to go with us on Sunday."

"Sunday?"

"Yes. Sunday. You know. The Academy Awards."

"You're kidding?"

"No. The lighting director's wife just had a baby this morning. He says he needs to be there when they go home from the hospital, so…"

"Charles, could we maybe talk about this another time? This really isn't a good—"

"We don't have that much time, Lil. It's only two days away." He looked up when he saw Tony come walking out of the bedroom, also in a hotel robe with slightly disheveled hair. "Oh."

"Hello, Charles," Tony said as politely as he could muster. He strolled up behind Lily and wound his arms around her. He kissed her on the neck for the sheer satisfaction of watching Charles squirm.

Charles refused to oblige. Instead, he looked Tony dead in the eyes with a crooked little smile. "Hello. Tony," he said. "Glad to see the *situation* hasn't slowed you down." He sounded strangely smug.

"Hmm. And I'm very glad to see that you've been apprised of the *situation*." Tony gave Lily a sarcastic grin.

"Tony," she said in a cautionary tone.

"What? Don't you think it's odd?"

"Like I said, word gets around," Charles said again, this time with a know-it-all air.

"How?" Tony said.

"I'll give you one guess," Charles said, making eye contact with Lily.

Lily sighed. "Initials C.C.?"

Charles smiled.

"I should have known," Lily said.

"Who?" Tony said.

"Channing," Charles said.

"Nice! The good doctor immediately called him to share the news about my case? That's not illegal or anything," he said.

"No! Not Eric," Lily assured him. "His wife— Cecily Channing—she answered the phone the other day when I called."

"At his office?" Tony said.

"No. I called his home phone. I didn't think to swear her to secrecy.

"It wouldn't have done any good," Charles added with a chuckle.

"True! Anyway, I'm sure she couldn't wait to call Charles to share the news."

"About me?" Tony asked.

"No," Lily said. "About me. The same way my brother messaged you to report that your ex-girlfriend was pregnant. For the same reason that you still follow her on Facebook and like pictures of her baby—the one you didn't want to tell me about. It's human nature to want to know what happens to people we care about. Even when we've moved on with other people."

That stopped Tony. Charles, who'd been watching the show, smiled with some degree of satisfaction.

"So, anyway," Charles said, "Lil, I thought you might also like to know that Robert Mitchell is going to be there. He hasn't hired anyone yet, so if you still have any interest in doing that special, it would give you a chance to connect."

Lily looked skeptical.

"I can have Morgan rustle something up for you."

"On such short notice?"

"Trust me."

"Who's Morgan?" Tony said.

"Our stylist," Lily said. "Charles, I really didn't come to L.A. to—"

"Just think about it," Charles said. "Think about it and call me. Tonight." Then, glancing at Tony, he added snidely, "If you can tear yourself away for a minute."

Tony wasn't sure if he was supposed to be offended, but he stood a little taller as he stared him down.

"Later, Tony," Charles said as he headed for the door.

The door closed behind Charles. Tony remained silent.

"Ugh!" Lily walked past him and into the bedroom.

He followed her. "Lil, about Tracie..."

"Tony—"

"I can explain," Tony said.

"Explain what? He's not yours, is he?"

"What? Why would you even ask me that?"

"I did the math. He's about six months old, which means she probably conceived sometime in November. Correct me if I'm wrong, but I believe the two of you were sleeping together until just before Thanksgiving, weren't you?"

"Yes, but—"

"Well, then, there you go. It's possible, isn't it?"

"Yes. It is possible. But he's not mine. Do you really think I'd have a child and not tell you?"

She didn't answer.

He approached her and put a hand on her shoulder. "That's not the reason I didn't mention it."

"I know that." She shook him off and walked back into the sitting room.

"Do you?"

"Of course," she said firmly. "You didn't tell me because you didn't think I could handle it. You thought I would lose my shit if I found out she got pregnant. If I knew she had a baby when I can't."

It was an accurate assessment, and based on her reaction, he thought he'd made the right choice. But as much as he thought she sometimes needed to be handled with kid gloves, he knew she hated to be. "How did you hear about it?" he asked.

"I saw some pictures on Danny's page." She bit her lip. "Aaron. That's his name, isn't it? He's a beautiful little boy," she said with a quiver in her voice.

"Lily," he said. "I should have told you, but—"

"I'm not upset about that."

"You're not?"

"No!" she said with renewed anger. "I'm upset because of the scene you just caused with Charles."

"The scene *I* caused with Charles? He barges in here and interrupts us in the middle of making love and I'm the one who caused a scene?"

"Yes! I could have got rid of him and come back to bed. No problem. But you had to come out here and assert your masculinity, prove you had me and he didn't, and accuse him of some kind of foul play. For God's sake!"

"He obviously still wants you!"

"So what if he does? When are you going to get it through your skull? It doesn't matter what he does. I left him for you. I divorced him for you. I want you! Can't you see that? He's not a threat to us anymore. The only thing threatening us right now is cancer!"

Tony still saw Charles as more of a threat than she did, but she was right about one thing. Cancer was a bigger one. He moved to put his arms around her again and she tried to swat him away until he grabbed her fists and pulled her to him. He held her so tightly she couldn't move to break free.

"I'm sorry, sweetheart," he whispered. "I don't want to fight with you."

"I don't want to fight with you either," she said through her tears.

He eased her over to the sofa and sat. She curled up on his lap.

"I'm sorry too," she said. "I promised myself I wouldn't dwell on it this weekend. That we could just enjoy each other without... and already I..." She shook her head at a loss for words again.

Tony tenderly stroked her hair for a few minutes before he spoke again. "I think I know how we can make it up to each other."

"You do?"

"Yes."

"You want to make love again?"

"No. Well... a bit later perhaps." He laughed. "Actually I was thinking about something else."

"What's that?"

"I think we should go to the ceremony on Sunday."

"What? Who are you and what *have* you done with my Tony?"

"I'm serious."

She gave him a sideways glance that demanded an explanation.

"See, I'll agree to play nice with Charles to prove to you I'm secure in our relationship and you can schmooze with Robert Mitchell and land the Christmas special to prove to me that you aren't going to let my situation keep you from living your life. What do you think of that?"

She thought for a minute. "I *have* always wanted to do a Christmas special."

"Right."

"And it only takes a couple of days to film anyway."

"So it wouldn't even need to be a long-term commitment," he said.

"There is still the matter of a dress," she said, starting to sound more upbeat.

"What?"

"For Sunday."

"All the more reason to go shopping," Tony chuckled.

"Good Lord, I can't buy off the rack for the Oscars. That would be unheard of! It's practically professional suicide," she laughed.

Tony laughed with her as if he'd known all along it was a ridiculous idea.

"But with two days—I'm not sure even Morgan can work that kind of miracle."

"Charles sounded certain," Tony said.

"Charles always sounds certain."

"Is that what attracted you too him? His confidence and take-charge attitude?"

Lily leaned her head back and eyed him.

"I'm joking," Tony chuckled. "I should never ask questions I don't really want to know the answers to."

She shook her head at him.

"What?" he said innocently.

"Forget it. We're not going."

"Why?"

"Because I don't think it's going to work. How are you ever going to get through an entire evening with him?"

"Oh, don't worry. I'm sure I'll be too distracted by your incomparable beauty to notice him."

"Is that so?"

"Absolutely," he said, nuzzling her neck.

"And what are you envisioning? Something in black, maybe? Or gold!"

"I think I prefer you in red!"

"Oh, no! To match the carpet?" she laughed.

"Ha! I guess that would be odd, wouldn't it?"

"Quite."

"Well, how about blue? I like you in blue."

"Perhaps."

"But I think I prefer you out of it!"

"I'm sure we can arrange something."

"You think so?"

"I do."

"So accommodating! That's why I love you," Tony said. He kissed her nose.

"I love you more," she said, snuggling into him. "If you're lucky, I may let you kiss me on the red carpet."

He heard the smile return to her voice. He sat there cradling her for quite some time. After a while, he asked her if she was ready to go back to bed. When she didn't answer, he realized she'd already fallen asleep.

Tony managed to get off of the sofa and carry Lily into the bedroom. He laid her gently on the bed and tucked the covers up around her chin. She stirred, but quickly adjusted to her new surroundings. He removed his robe and crawled in next to her, saying a silent prayer that neither cancer nor Charles would destroy them. He allowed the rhythm of her breathing and the warmth of her body to lull him to sleep.

8
PARTY ON

"And the award goes to..." A hush fell over the Dolby Auditorium as the presenter fumbled with the envelope.

"Say it already," Charles thought. His heart was pounding in his chest.

Lily gave his hand a gentle squeeze and he took a breath. Then he heard it.

"C.S. George for *Avengers of Athena*."

"Fuck yeah!" he mouthed as he sprung from his chair.

Without thinking he turned toward Lily.

"You did it!" she said as she threw her arms around him.

"Yes!" he said as he hugged her, lifting her completely off the ground. Suddenly he remembered. Cora. "Shit," he said and turned to her next.

After another hug and a quick kiss on the cheek he was off and headed for the stage, dodging the seat-filler who was waiting to take his place.

"Fuck yeah!" he thought again as he dashed up the aisle. The star-studded crowd on either side was a blur as he hurried by them, all the while re-writing his acceptance speech in his head for about the fourteenth time.

He reached the stage and took the steps two at a time. He held the statue for a moment before speaking, admiring its golden beauty, marveling at the weight of it in his hand.

"I don't care how many of these you get your hands on, it's still hard to get used to," he said. He paused for laughter from the crowd. "I was so excited to get my hands on this one, I almost pulled a Benigni."

Another laugh from the crowd—at least from those who'd been around long enough to remember Roberto Benigni seat-surfing after his win for *Life is Beautiful*.

Out in the house, Tony chuckled too as he shifted in his seat. He had to admit that Charles had a certain charm about him, but that was an admission he'd keep to himself. He looked at Lily. She was calm, relaxed, smiling. She'd amazed him on the red carpet that evening. She was breath-taking in her strapless, organza gown—a vision in watercolor African violet. And the way she'd handled the questions, some of them pointed, and the cameras—so natural and confident. She was in her element, he thought. He turned his attention back to Charles just as he was finishing thanking his cast and crew.

"And now, to my friends and family," Charles went on. "Cora, you are invaluable to me. I hope you know that. To you, my sister Gladys, and especially... Lizzie..."

"Who's Lizzie?" Tony heard Cora ask, leaning around the seat-filler to address Lily.

Lily didn't answer. She stared intently at the stage as Charles went on.

"Thank you for your love and support—for putting up with the early mornings and the late nights, the attitude and the inattention. Thank you for allowing... and forgiving... what it takes to be me and to do what I do."

He paused and looked directly into the monitor as soft music began to filter through the auditorium.

"There goes the music," he said. "Just let me say it once more before they play me off. For this... and for all for all of the other times I never said it... I love you. Thank you!"

As applause erupted again and Charles made his way off stage, Tony glanced at Lily.

She swallowed, inconspicuously blotted a tear from the corner of her eye, and resumed smiling and applauding.

* * *

Just a few levels up from the auditorium, the ballroom buzzed with energy and excitement as the losers, presenters, and others awaited the arrival of the night's big winners. As they entered, Lily reminded Tony, "Don't forget to smile. You never know what's going to be caught on film."

"Ha! I'll try," he said. He'd taken about three steps when she tightened her hold on his elbow.

"Wait," Lily cautioned.

He paused as instructed and several flashbulbs went off.

"Good Lord. This is not my life," he laughed.

"Relax. You'll be fine," she said as they began to make their way through the crowd. "Just be yourself. Everyone loves you."

"I don't know about that. Not here anyway."

"Well, I do. That's all that really matters." She squeezed his arm. "Now, let's *mingle*, shall we?"

He gave her a quick kiss on the cheek and put on a nice smile. "Let's do it."

They worked their way through the room. Tony hung back, allowing Lily to meet, greet and schmooze to her heart's content. It wasn't his scene—big dresses, big hair, heavy make-up, everyone pretending to be what others wanted them to be—but Lily was obviously having a marvelous time. So, he smiled and nodded and answered when spoken to, but he was never so happy to be handed a drink in all his life.

Lily looked concerned as he took the first healthy swallow. "Is that a good idea?" she said.

"One won't hurt and this is damn good stuff," he said, taking another swallow. "I'll say one thing for Hollywood. People here throw one a hell of a party."

"True," she laughed. "That's our specialty!"

Tony was putting on a good show, but Lily knew he was on edge. He was unusually quiet and more self-conscious than she'd ever seen him. Whether it was the festivities or Charles's impending reappearance, she wasn't sure. She spotted Cora and was headed in her direction when a voice boomed over the crowd.

"Lillian George!"

"Oh, here we go!" Lily said aloud to no one in particular.

Seconds later, Michael Marinello was practically on top of her.

"How are you, gorgeous?" he asked, planting a kiss on her cheek.

"Hello Michael, darling. I'm fine. How are you?" She turned her head and he kissed the other cheek too. "Great job up there tonight."

"Ah, nothing to it," Michael said. Then, turning to Tony, he asked, "Do I know you?"

"Ah, Michael, this is Tony Ward." There it was again, she thought—that awkward moment. My boyfriend?

"Tony Ward?" Michael questioned as he shook his hand. "Oh! Right! You're the one who stole her away from the great Charles George."

Lily could see Tony's face contort as he tried to swallow those words.

71

"Actually—" Tony started to say.

"What's next on your agenda, Michael?" she asked before Tony could finish his response. "Anything new in the works?"

"Oh, yeah. I've got a few things coming down the pipe. But I'll tell you what's on my agenda for tonight—besides the cute blonde at the bar—"

"Oh, Lord. What's that?"

"Dancing!" He did a little wiggle.

"Really?"

"Oh yeah. With you!" He took her hands and spun her into an awkward cradle hold, throwing her off balance.

"Ha ha! Well, we'll have to see about that," she said as she back led her way out of the hold. "Would you excuse us, please?"

"Sure. Good to see you," he said, with a wink.

"Yes, you too." She gave him a slight wave as she and Tony walked away.

In the far corner of the room, they found Cora chatting with a pretty, young blonde who turned out to be Marinello's flavor of the week. "I'd love to meet Mr. George," the woman was saying.

"Where is the man of the hour, anyway?" Tony asked.

"He should be here soon. The press room business takes a while, you know," Lily said.

"Hmm," Tony said.

"Speaking of which... Cora, why don't we grab a table, hmm? You know how Charles likes to hold court."

"He does? Oh, right. He does," Cora said.

Lily floated over to the nearest high-top and put her drink down to stake her claim.

Tony caught the uneasy look on Cora's face as she followed Lily.

Moments later, C.S. George swept into the ballroom with a golden statue in one hand and a glass of champagne in the other. Tony surveyed the room. The blonde swooned, star-struck. Cora wrung her hands and only managed a smile when she realized he was looking at her. Charles moved confidently through the throngs of admirers, flashbulbs lighting his path, and Lily never took her eyes off of him.

"Congratulations," she said when he reached them. "I'm so proud of you!"

He leaned in and folded the Oscar and the glass around her as she hugged him. "Thanks!" he said. "I'm so glad that you could join us tonight." He paused and held the statue out to Cora expectantly.

Cora took it rather reluctantly.

Charles picked up Lily's glass and handed it to her. "Here's to... peace, love, and friendship, huh?" He raised his glass.

"And success!" she said as she raised hers. She and Charles instinctively paused for the picture they knew was coming. Tony and Cora shared an uncomfortable smile and belatedly joined the toast.

"Okay," Charles said after gulping down his champagne. "I've had my moment. Now it's time for you to have yours."

"What are you talking about?" Lily said, surprised by his uncharacteristic solicitude.

Charles put an arm around her and turned her toward the other side of the room. "Do you see who I see?" he said.

"Mitchell?"

"Exactly." He led her away.

Tony shook his head as he watched Lily and Charles huddle together. "Tell me, Miss Barker," Tony asked, "are you enjoying this evening as much as I am?"

"Please, call me Cora," she said. "Is it that obvious?" she asked, having detected the hint of sarcasm in his question.

"Only occasionally."

"Sorry."

"No need to apologize."

"This just really isn't my scene, you know? I'm more of a behind the scenes party planner. Lily was always the one who..." Cora sighed.

"Knew how to work a crowd?" Tony said.

Cora nodded. "Exactly. She lights up a room."

"That she does."

"She handles everything and everyone with such grace. She knows what Charles expects, what he wants. And he... I shouldn't be saying any of this to you."

"It's all right. Look at this way. It's only a few more hours, right?"

"For you, maybe. For me... this is my life now." She laughed nervously. "I love Charles, but sometimes I don't think I'm cut out for this side of things."

"Mmm," Tony said. "I know I'm not."

"To tell you the truth, I don't think I'll ever be able to fill those shoes. I don't know if anyone can," Cora said, her eyes still trained on Lily.

"I know what you mean," Tony said, though more to himself than to Cora. He exhaled as he watched Charles whisper something in Lily's ear.

Meanwhile, in the huddle, Lily asked Charles, "What do you think I should say to him? I mean, what do you suppose the best angle is with him?"

"I don't think you should say anything. I think you need to let your moves speak for themselves."

"Charles!"

"On the dance floor, woman! Keep it out of the gutter!" he teased.

Lily laughed and gave him a shove.

"Well? What are you waiting for? Don't look at me. Go get your partner."

Lily sailed back to the table with Charles close behind. "How's it going over here?" she asked, seeing the less-than-thrilled looks on their faces.

"Oh, just fine," Tony said. "Cora and I were just... commiserating."

"About what?" Charles asked.

"Never mind. What were you two conferring about?" Tony said.

"Mitchell is here," Lily said, her hands clutched in front of herself.

"So I heard," Tony said. "Are you going to go talk to him?"

"No. I need you."

"I don't think I'd be much help."

"Of course you will. I want to give him a preview. I need you to dance with me."

"Oh! I see. And what do I get out of this deal?" he asked playfully.

"You get to dance with me," she said with a wink. Then she stepped in closer. "And when we get back to the hotel..." she whispered, "you get to do anything and everything else you want with me."

"Well, when you put it like that, what are we waiting for?"

"I'll clear the way for you," Charles said. "What are you going to do?"

Lily considered it for about half a second and said, "Best Original Song. 'Skyfall.'"

"You got it," Charles said, and he headed over to the sound booth.

"'Skyfall?'" Tony said.

"Yes. We do like a Contemporary-infused Bolero. Start with some simple lifts—attitude, fish, hip lift. Work your way up to a shoulder sit and finish with a dip."

"Something like that Contemporary *Swan Lake* number you were working on?"

"Exactly."

"Can you do it in that dress?"

A grin washed over her face. "Just wait until you see what this dress can do," she said. "Come on." She grabbed his hand and tugged him toward a darkened corner. She unfastened her belt and peeled off the flowing, full-length skirt to reveal a knee-length sheer one beneath it, covering what he now realized was a form-fitting, U-necked body suit.

"That is fabulous," he said.

"Isn't it? Charles—and Morgan—had it specially made."

"Are you sure we can do this here?" Tony asked as he removed his tuxedo jacket and tie.

"Ladies and gentlemen, we have a special treat for you tonight," a voice boomed out over the sound system. "Dancing to tonight's Oscar-winning song, please welcome the incomparable Lily Josephson and her partner Tony Ward."

"Does that answer your question?" she said. She finished unbuttoning his shirt and slipped off her shoes.

"Bloody hell," he said. "When did we join the cast of *Dancing with the Stars*?"

"Ha! You're not backing out on me, are you?"

"No. But you just might owe me for this one!"

"Fair enough. Let's go!"

As he followed her barefoot onto the dance floor, he couldn't help thinking about how far she'd come since that night he first dragged her out onto the floor—her first live performance after the accident. He'd had to promise her that he would be there to catch her if she fell. Tonight, with the celebrities and cameras everywhere, he rather hoped she'd be there to catch him.

As Lily and Tony took to the floor, Cora and Charles watched from their table at the edge of it.

"They look beautiful together, don't they?" she asked.

"Beautiful."

"Just look at the way they look at each other. Like they're the only two people in the world. So raw. So real. Even in the middle of... this," she said with a wave of her hand.

Charles said nothing, but he found himself wishing, maybe for the first time ever, that he were the one out on that floor.

"Are you okay?" Cora asked him.

"Sure. Why wouldn't I be? I'm the one who told her to do it."

They watched for another minute without speaking, until Cora broke the silence again. "I wish I had even a tenth of her style," she said.

Charles looked at her puzzled for a moment then put an arm around her shoulder. "Hey, baby... you have style."

"Not like her."

"You're different people. You're both wonderful. Just... different," he said. He kissed the top of her head and pulled her closer.

Lily and Tony made their way back through the crowd that had gathered around the table.

"Man, that was hot! I got some great shots of you two!" Marinello called. He held up his phone as if he had some kind of prize.

"Let me see them," Charles said.

Michael passed him the phone and he and Cora examined them, deciding which ones were Twitter-worthy.

"Oh, God," Tony said under his breath.

"Sorry, but it is great publicity," Lily said, patting his cheek.

"I feel so used," Tony joked.

"Can you ever forgive me?" Lily winked at him.

"I'll let you know."

"Let's see if the plan worked. Here comes Robert now," Charles said.

"Lily!"

"Hello Robert!" Lily said. She took a few steps away from the table, still holding Tony's hand. "Tony, this is the producer/director I was telling you about. Robert, Tony Ward."

"Nice to meet you. You're one lucky man."

"I am indeed." He raised her hand to his lips and kissed it.

"Well, Lily," Mitchell said, "when Charles suggested I give you a shot at choreographing the special, I was skeptical. I mean, no offense sweetie... I wasn't sure if you were still up to it. But after seeing that, there is no longer any question in my mind. You're obviously as good as ever. Maybe better. I'd love to see what you can do with a little planning time and a full cast. That show is yours if you want it."

"Just like that?" Lily said, surprised.

"Just like that," Robert repeated.

"Oh, Robert, that's wonderful. Thank you. I'd love it!"

"Great! Hell, I may just put you in front of the camera, too. What do you say?"

She looked at Tony, who gave a small nod. "Yes!" she said. "Absolutely!"

"For that matter, what about you, Tony? Ever done any camera work?"

"Oh, no! I'm an architect."

"Yeah, sure, but you're also a dancer. Clearly."

"My parents were dancers," Tony said.

Robert ignored the clarification. "With your chemistry and looks, the two of you could really haul in the ladies in the thirty-plus market."

"Wouldn't Maggie and Joe love that?" Lily laughed. "Robert, it is a very interesting offer," Lily said. "We will keep it in mind."

"I wouldn't hold my breath, though, if I were you," Tony added.

"Can't blame me for trying. I'll have my assistant fax over the paperwork in the morning. Where are you staying?"

"We're at the Wilshire," Lily said.

"Fine. Talk to you soon, doll."

"Great! Thanks, Robert." She said. She waited until Robert had walked away before throwing her arms around Tony's neck. "We did it!" she squealed.

"*You* did it!" he reminded her as he scooped her into his arms.

She leaned back to look at his face. "Are you ready to get out of here?"

"I thought you'd never ask."

"Let's just say our goodbyes, then," she said, leading him toward Charles and Cora.

"Hey," Charles said, perking up as they approached. "Can I get you another drink?" Then he added, "Either of you?"

"No, thank you," Tony said.

"Actually, we just came over to say good night," Lily said.

"You're not leaving, are you? So soon?" Charles said. "We were just about to head over to the Tower for the Fair."

Tony gave Lily a questioning look.

"The big *Vanity Fair* party at the Sunset Tower Hotel," she explained. "All the A-Listers end up there. Or at least they stop there."

"Oh. Well, we can go if you want to," Tony said.

She *did* want to go, but Tony had suffered enough already, so she declined politely and started gathering the pieces of her dress and her shoes.

"But what about our midnight toast?" Charles said. "You've always led a midnight toast with the cast ever since we..." He

81

stopped and looked at her and then at Tony, as if reality had just jumped up and smacked him in the face.

Lily licked her lips and smiled sweetly, then said, "I think... maybe that's someone else's job now." She placed a hand on Cora's shoulder.

"Oh, no!" Cora blurted out.

Charles looked sideways at her.

"Sorry, but that's not me. I've never... I could never..."

"You'll figure it out," Lily said. "I have faith in you. In both of you."

"I'll call James to take you back," Charles said. He set his drink down and pulled his phone out.

"You don't have to do that," Lily said. "We can—"

"No. It's no trouble. He can come back for us," Charles said.

"Are you sure?" Lily said.

"Absolutely." He quickly placed the call while Lily and Cora hugged and said their good-byes. He shook Tony's hand and wished him luck, then turned one last time to Lily.

"Will I see you again before you leave?" he asked as he hugged her.

"Ah, I don't know," Lily said, gasping a bit, surprised by the force with which he swept her into his arms. He lingered long enough that she finally felt obligated to pull away. Even then, he still held on to her hands.

"Will you keep me—us— posted? Let us know what happens on Tuesday? I mean, if you think about it."

Lily glanced back at Tony, who shrugged his approval.

"Sure," she said as she slowly backed away, freeing herself from his grip. Her fingers reached back for Tony's hand, which was ready and waiting.

Tony gave a nod, and with that, they turned and walked away.

Charles rested an elbow on the table and watched as they crossed the room and disappeared through the door on the other side, then reached for his drink and took a swig.

"You still love her, don't you?" Cora said.

Charles was shocked, but impressed by her candor. His eyes darted in her direction and then refocused on the exit just as quickly. He took a breath and blew it out forcefully through his nose. He took another drink and crunched through an ice cube.

"Charles?" Cora prodded.

"Don't make me answer that. Please," he said. He pushed off of the table and walked away.

* * *

Tony sat in the refuge of the town car, relieved to be out of the limelight and happy to be headed back to the solitude of the Wilshire Hotel. Lily, on the other hand, didn't seem happy at all. She was quiet, gazing out the window at the passing palms for most of the ride. Eventually, Tony reached for her hand.

"Hey, there. Are you all right?"

She turned and smiled one of those tight-lipped, I'm-hiding-something smiles. "Of course. Why wouldn't I be?"

"Oh, I don't know. Maybe you wish you'd worn the Gucci earrings instead of Dior, you know. They might have been more noticeable in the dance floor photos."

No reaction.

"Or, maybe you're upset because Marinello's girlfriend was obviously ogling me with my shirt open. But I don't want you to worry about that at all. I mean maybe, if it had been Kate Winslet or—"

"She's got bigger feet than you'd expect, doesn't she?" Lily said absent-mindedly.

"Who?"

"Kate Winslet. They're size eleven."

"Oh," he said. Then, after a pause he asked, "Do you miss it? This life? Him?"

She thought for a moment, nibbling her bottom lip. "Yes," she said quietly. "Sometimes."

He looked down and swallowed.

"But I have something better now," she said. "Something I want more."

He looked up at her again.

"I've got you." She leaned over and kissed him, a good, long, open-mouthed kiss that left him temporarily speechless. "And I got a job! Thanks to you," she grinned.

"You got a job because you're an amazing performer and a talented choreographer."

She smiled wider. "Yes. I am," she said, sitting up straighter.

He wound an arm around her waist and scooted her closer to him. "You are an amazing woman, Lily Josephson," he whispered as he nuzzled her neck. "I'm so very proud of you. Of everything you've accomplished. And I love you. Je t'aime de tout mon coeur."

"Mmm. Je t'aime aussi, mon cher. I don't know what I would ever do without you," she said.

He could feel the curve of her lips as she smiled against his cheek.

"I don't know," he said. "But if I have any say in the matter, you'll never have to find out."

"I'm going to hold you to that," she said, still silently hoping that God and the universe had the same idea.

9
STRIKE TWO

Lily paced around Eric Channing's office. She examined the framed degrees and family portraits on the walls, looking for any way to distract herself.

"You can sit, you know, darling." Tony said.

"Sorry," she said. She sat reluctantly on the edge of the chair. "It's just being here... in the office... waiting for news..."

"Don't tell me my impatience is starting to wear off on you," Tony said with a little chuckle.

Lily looked away for a moment, then back again. "I think I should tell you something," she said. "About Eric... ah... Dr. Channing."

"You're biting your lip again. Should I be alarmed?" Tony said.

"No. But—"

Before Lily could finish her statement, the door opened.

"Sorry to keep you waiting," Dr. Channing said as he walked in. "I wanted to call in a consult from another colleague, just to be sure." He stopped in front of Lily and she rose to greet him. "Lillian, you look well," he said. He kissed her on the cheek.

"Thank you. So do you," Lily said. "And thank you so much for seeing us."

"I'm glad I was able to fit you in," the doctor said. He greeted Tony and shook his hand before taking his place behind the large desk and opening Tony's file.

Lily sat and reached for Tony's hand.

"So, what's the verdict?" Tony asked.

"I wish I had better news."

"I don't think I like the sound of that," Tony said.

"Neither do I," Channing said. "There's no easy way to say this type of thing."

The knot that seemed to have taken up residence in Lily's stomach constricted again. She met Tony's eyes. He held tighter to her hand.

"I have both sets of scans here. The first set is what Dr. Branson sent me. The second set is the bunch that we took this morning. As you can see, there is a small mass here where the original tumor was removed, so either they didn't get it all the first time or we have a rapid recurrence. By the looks of it, we also have an affected lymph node here, which we're going to have to deal with. What bothers me most is this spot over here on the left kidney."

"What is that? Another tumor?" Tony asked.

"I'm afraid so."

Lily cleared her throat to stifle a sob.

Tony exhaled. "So, what type of prognosis are we talking about? What method of treatment do you suggest?" Tony asked.

"At this point I don't think we have much choice but to remove the right kidney entirely. As for the left, I'm hopeful that it can be salvaged. I would remove only that portion of tissue, leaving the organ viable. As long as it still functions properly, you should be able to live a normal, healthy life."

"Is there a chance that it would not function properly?" Tony said.

"There is always a chance. If the area we remove turns out to be more than what we are expecting, it could cause a problem."

"Then what?"

"Worst-case scenario?" The doctor hesitated.

Tony leaned forward in his chair, now cupping Lily's hand between both of his.

"We could be looking at dialysis."

Tony's face fell.

"But we are hopeful it won't come to that," Channing said.

"Are there any other options?" Tony said.

"Not as far as I'm concerned. With the speed at which this appears to be spreading, I wouldn't risk any alternative. It's an aggressive cancer. We need to take aggressive action."

"What about chemo or radiation instead of surgery?" Lily said.

"Radiation and chemo are less effective when dealing with this type of cancer, but we would follow the procedure with targeted therapy to attack anything we might have missed and prevent any further recurrence. Immunotherapy may also be an option."

Lily and Tony looked thoughtfully at one another.

"What are you thinking?" Tony asked her.

"It doesn't sound like there's much *to* think about, is there?"

"What kind of time frame are we looking at here? When would you schedule the surgery?"

"Well, I understand that you weren't originally coming to me for anything but a second opinion about follow-up treatment. But if you were one of my family members, I wouldn't let you leave this office without having it arranged. I don't think we can't afford to wait with this one. Fortunately, I had a cancellation earlier. I should be able to fit you on the schedule Friday afternoon."

Lily's mouth fell open. "Friday?"

Tony blew out a slow breath.

Channing looked back and forth between the two of them. "Why don't I give you two a moment alone to process all of this? I'll check the surgical schedule to be certain someone hasn't stolen my spot."

"Thank you, doctor," Tony said as Channing rose from his seat.

"Of course," Channing nodded. "I'll be back in few minutes to see if you have any other questions."

The moment the doctor stepped out, Lily was out of her chair.

"Lily," Tony called.

She didn't respond. She crossed the room and stopped in front of the wall of book cases. She focused on the volumes of books on the shelves, her arms hugging her chest.

Tony stood and followed her. "Lily," he whispered as he took hold of her shoulders and gently turned her around to face him.

"I'm sorry," she said. "I just didn't expect..." She looked away and wiped a tear from the corner of her eye with her ring finger.

He pulled her into his embrace. "Darling, we knew this might not be easy, didn't we? But we said we would face it head on, right? So here it is. We're staring it in the face. What are we going do about it?"

She sighed. "What else can we do? The way it sounds, we don't have a lot of choice, do we? We thought we would get a second opinion and new scans so we could be sure the cancer was really gone. But it's not gone. It's back, and with a vengeance. Not really the news we'd hoped for, is it?" Lily said.

"No, it isn't. The question is... do we do as he says? Do we trust his professional opinion?" Tony asked.

Lily thought a moment then said, "I think so, yes."

Tony had done enough research on the man to know she was right. "Well, why wait, then," he said. "Let's get it over with. The sooner I can get this poison out of my body, the sooner I can recover and the sooner we can get on with the rest of our lives."

Lily nodded.

He held her close and closed his eyes, breathing in her scent, letting her presence calm him.

A few minutes later Dr. Channing returned. Tony agreed to go ahead with the surgery and the doctor went over the pre-op instructions with them. They walked out of his office quietly hand in hand.

* * *

In the cab on the way back to the hotel he pulled out his cell phone and stared at it. "I guess I should call my family, shouldn't I?"

"No sense in prolonging the inevitable," she said. She took her phone out, too, and started a search.

He exhaled. "Knowing my mother, she's going to want to be here."

"And your sister."

"Yes."

"Find out how soon they can leave. I've got a flight on United leaving Heathrow at ten twenty-five tomorrow morning, connecting at JFK, and arriving here at one thirty-three L.A. time and I can get them in at the Wilshire."

"Thank you, angel." He took her outstretched hand.

She nodded and smiled, swallowing hard.

He turned her hand over and kissed her palm. "What were you going to say about Channing earlier?"

"Hmm?" she said, still fiddling with the airline reservations on her phone.

"Before he came in, you said you had something to tell me."

"Oh. Well... It doesn't matter now."

"What was it?"

She hesitated. "I was just going to warn you that he's a real straight shooter who never sugar-coats anything. But you know that now, don't you?"

10
REINFORCEMENTS

On Friday afternoon, Lily paced in the waiting room, wringing her hands, fiddling with the ring on her right hand. It was after four o'clock and Tony's family still hadn't arrived.

She sent Danny a text.

- **Do you have a minute?**

When he didn't answer, she picked up a *Women's Health* magazine and perused it for about the third time. She found an article on stretching and made a mental note to add one of the stretches to her morning routine, then tossed the magazine back down on the table and stared at it for lack of anything more interesting to look at.

"Hey, Lil," she heard someone say.

She looked up. "Charles? What on earth are you doing here?"

"You never called me back."

She rolled her eyes. "Sorry. I've had a few other things on my mind."

"I know. I heard."

"How?"

"You told your brother. He told Nina. Nina told Cora, so…"

"They still keep in touch?"

"Pretty regularly. Anyway, I thought maybe you could use a real cup of coffee," he said. He held out the Starbucks cup he was holding.

She gave him a suspicious look and cautiously took the cup. "Thanks." She carefully peeled off the lid and peered inside.

"It's just black, no fancy stuff, but…"

"Oh, no, that's fine. Thank you," she said again. She replaced the top and took a sip.

He sat down next to her on the vinyl sofa and rubbed his palms on his thighs.

When he didn't say anything, she asked, "So, what did you need?"

"Nothing."

"Really?"

"Don't sound so shocked. I do occasionally think of others, you know. I thought you might not want to be alone. That's all."

A half smile appeared for a millisecond before she looked away.

"So what's the word?"

"There is no word yet."

Charles could hear the restrained emotion in her voice. He reached over and began to gently rub her back. She flinched and took a breath. He wondered if it was due to his touch or because she was struggling to keep from breaking down. He hoped it was the latter.

"Hey, Lil, it's gonna be okay."

"You don't know that."

"Look at me."

She shook her head.

"Look at me," he said again. He leaned forward to see her face.

She looked at him sideways.

"The first time I was in this hospital I was exactly where you are now. Only you were the patient. You'd just been brought in after the accident. Your pelvis was fractured, your spine was fractured, you were all torn up. They took you in to surgery immediately and I couldn't do anything but sit and wait. I didn't know if you would live and even if you did, I wondered if you would ever walk again. And then, after that, when you..." He stopped and shook his head.

Lily swallowed and turned to make full eye contact. The look in his eyes was one she'd rarely seen. Hearing him talk about the time after the accident was almost as painful for her as it was for him. "Charles—"

"What I'm saying is that things looked pretty bleak. But look at you now. Healthy. Strong. You fought through it. He will too. You'll see."

Lily couldn't take it anymore. Finally, overcome with emotion, she fell sideways into Charles and buried her face in his shoulder.

Charles glanced around the room, then put an arm around her and gave her a weak squeeze.

When his phone rang in his pocket, he jumped and she sat back up.

"You should get that," she sniffed.

"Don't worry about it."

"No, go ahead," she assured him.

He removed it from his jacket and checked the display. "Okay. Just a second."

She nodded and he stood.

"Hey Diane," he said. "Can this wait? I'm with Lillian right now, and I—"

Lily heard his agent's resounding, "No, it cannot wait!" through the phone.

Charles looked at her and she nodded again and waved him off. While she waited for him to come back, she fished her phone from her purse. Danny had answered.

- **Sorry, sweetie. Cam was in the middle of a tantrum. Any news?**
- Cam?
- **He plays Ricky. Any news?**
- Not yet.

She waited a moment and he answered again.

- **Did Anna and Maggie arrive safely?**
- Not yet.
- **Thought they were due in yesterday?**
- Nope. Anna had to wrap up a case in court.
- **I'm sorry. I wish I could be there with you. I hate thinking of you there alone.**
- I'm not alone.

- **???**
- Charles is here.
- **Oh?**
- He brought me coffee.

Before Danny could ask any more questions, Charles returned.

"Sorry about that," he said.

"It's okay. I was just..." She waved her phone around and then tossed it back into her bag. "Everything all right?"

"Why wouldn't it be?" he said.

Lily thought he sounded a touch defensive. She shrugged. "Diane sounded concerned. I thought maybe there was a problem."

"Diane is always concerned. That's what I pay her for."

"Hmm," she nodded.

"But, I do have to go. Are you going to be okay here?"

"Sure," she nodded. "You go ahead and go." She stood, intentionally holding her head up and pushing her shoulders back

Charles stretched out his arms and she walked into them.

"Thank you for coming," she said.

"Any time," he said, smiling over her shoulder. "If you need anything, you call me, okay?"

"Okay," she said obediently.

"Lily," a woman's voice said.

Charles let go and Lily looked up to find Tony's mother and sister at the door.

His sister and Lily rushed toward each other.

"I'm so sorry we didn't get here sooner," she said throwing her arms around Lily. "The flight was a little late and by the time we made it to the hotel and figured out what to do with the bags—"

"I wouldn't worry too much about it, Anna, dear," his mother said. She looked from Lily to Charles and back again. "It looks to me like Lily had plenty of support."

11
ROAD TO RECOVERY

Maggie Ward scowled for the next forty minutes until the nurse came to announce that Tony had been brought into recovery.

Once they were taken back to see him, she moved from scowling to fretting. Anna tried to comfort her, reminding her that no one had ever looked particularly dapper following major surgery. But the only thing that seemed to calm her was fussing over him. So, Lily, Maggie, and Anna spent the next several hours pampering Tony while he floated in and out of sleep. Lily and Anna let Maggie do most of it, knowing that Maggie wouldn't have had it any other way.

Lily sat quietly on the sofa in the corner of Tony's room watching the two of them. As much as she knew he probably hated all of the attention, she also thought it nice that he had such a caring and concerned family. It was not a luxury she or her brother had ever had. But just as she was envying him his family, he stirred and let out a slight groan. Lily could just hear his voice urging them to stop hovering. She wondered if his crinkled features were signs of his reaction to being "under surveillance," as he sometimes called it. He was a very private person in spite of his strong familial relationships.

Truthfully, Lily was, too, sharing her innermost thoughts with very few people, but she'd gotten used to being watched long ago. She'd had to. Show business, after all, was not meant for those who wished to avoid the limelight.

About an hour into their fluff, tuck and refresh rotations, her phone buzzed with a text notification.

After several exchanges, she paused and glanced up.

Tony appeared to be resting comfortably. Anna flipped through a magazine while Maggie sat silently, arms folded, staring at the various monitors as if she knew what they all meant.

Lily watched Maggie for a moment, smiling calmly just in case she happened to look over. She didn't. In fact, she appeared to be actively avoiding it. They had been so close once, but that was before. Before the break up. Before all of the misunderstandings. Before Charles. Now that she and Tony had reconciled, Lily prayed that she and Maggie might be friends again, but right now their closeness was no more than a distant memory.

When another message came in, she looked at her phone. "Holy shit!" she exclaimed.

"What's wrong?" Anna asked.

"Nothing," Lily said, still in shock. "It's good news, actually."

"From whom? Your ex-husband?" Maggie snipped.

"No," Lily said defensively.

"Mother!" Anna said simultaneously.

"It's from Agnes, my agent," Lily went on. "About the Christmas contract."

"Oh, super! So, just business as usual?" Maggie said.

Anna put a hand on her mother's arm.

"What's that supposed to mean?" Lily asked.

"Nothing," Maggie shrugged. "I'm very glad you're able to keep working while my son is lying here."

"Mother!" Anna said again. "He's sleeping. What do you want her to do? Stare at the monitors and watch his blood pressure the entire time? You're doing enough of that for everyone."

"I don't think I like your tone, Anna."

"I'm sorry, mum, but... Look, I'm worried about him too. So is Lily."

"Is she?"

"What?" Anna said.

"Look at her. Cavorting with her ex-husband, chatting away on her mobile all day, hmm?"

"Oh, for God's sake!" Lily said, springing to her feet. "Don't be ridiculous, Maggie!" she whispered through clenched teeth.

"I'm just pointing out what I saw," Maggie said.

"Charles brought me coffee. He sat with me until you arrived. What you saw... was one friend comforting another. That's all."

"Are you sure about that?"

Lily took a deep breath. She looked from Maggie to Anna. Anna's face was apologetic.

"I think I need to get some air."

"That's probably a good idea. It is a bit thick in here," Maggie snapped.

Lily rolled her eyes. "You'll call me if he wakes up again?" she said to Anna.

Anna nodded.

Lily stepped into the hallway and fell against the wall with a sigh. Her eyes closed, she heard him before she saw him.

"Everything okay?" he asked with a hand on her shoulder.

"Oh. Eric!" Lily said.

"I'm sorry if I startled you."

"It's fine.

"Is Tony awake?"

"He was. He's resting again now."

"Good." Dr. Channing leaned against the wall next to her, observing her. "Well, you can tell him I said the surgery went well and that Dr. Jones and Dr. Douglas agree. We're going to keep him a little longer than usual, just to keep an eye on him. Given that we also removed a piece of the second kidney, we want to be sure there are no complications. But if all goes well, he should be out of here in about a week."

"Thank you. I'm sure he'll be happy to hear that. I'm... happy to hear that. Relieved."

"The fight isn't over yet. You know that?"

"I know. But it's a start. I'm so glad that you were able to take his case. Thank you again for that. And for scrubbing in this afternoon."

"You're welcome. But I'm really just doing my job."

"Still."

"What about you. How are you doing?"

She gave him a sideways glare. His face was solemn. "I'm fine," she said.

"Are you sure?"

"It's been almost eight years, Eric."

"I realize that."

"So, no worries, all right?" she said.

"Good," he nodded.

They shared a smile and Channing excused himself. Lily followed him to the elevator and said good-bye. She stopped in the lounge to check her voicemail. She called Agnes and then headed back toward Tony's room.

Maggie met her half way down the hallway.

"What's going on?" Lily asked, bracing herself for a potential attack.

"He's awake."

Without a word, Lily picked up the pace. Maggie matched her stride and cut her off in front of the door.

"Wait," Maggie said.

"I'd really like to see him," Lily said.

"I need to say something first."

Lily sighed. "What is it?"

Maggie paused.

Lily attempted to move past her.

"I'm sorry." Maggie said.

Lily stared at her.

"I ah... I'm sorry."

"Is that all?"

"No." Maggie paused again. "It was wrong of me to assume that there was anything untoward going on before. But given your history—"

Lily stopped her. "Maggie, I appreciate the apology." Such as it was, she thought. "But if there's more to this conversation, could we perhaps have it some other time?"

Maggie nodded. "Of course."

Lily read the concern lingering in Maggie's eyes. "I love your son," she said. "And he loves me. And that's all you or anybody else needs to know."

"I just don't want to see him get hurt again," Maggie said.

"Well, that's good. Because I have no intention of hurting him." Lily stared at Maggie, her eyes watery, but firm.

Maggie swallowed and stepped aside.

Much more alert than before, Tony smiled widely at the sight of Lily. He and Anna exchanged a knowing look.

"We'll be back," Anna whispered to him.

"Thank you," he mouthed.

Lily watched Anna leave, taking Maggie with her.

Tony patted the bed next to him.

Lily rushed to his bedside and took his outstretched hand. She sat gently on the edge of the bed.

"How are you feeling?"

"Better than I expected."

"That'll be the drugs," Lily laughed.

"Or the company," Tony said. He brought her hand to his lips and kissed it.

Lily laughed again, still amazed and amused at how easily he could make her blush.

"What?"

"Nothing," she said. She kissed him on the corner of his mouth and sat back to look at him. Before she could stop it, a tear trickled down her cheek. She quickly wiped it away.

"Do I look that bad?" he said.

"No! You look good," she said, just happy to see him awake and talking.

"For a guy with one kidney," he teased.

"Ha! Well, yes. By those standards, you look great. Bloody gorgeous, come to think of it."

Tony started to laugh, but stopped when the post-op pain kicked in. "Don't make me laugh," he said.

"Sorry," she said with a sympathetic smile.

"So, Anna said you heard from Agnes?" he said.

"Oh, yes. But we don't need to talk about that right now. I spoke with Eric earlier... ah... Dr. Channing."

"Lily..."

"Don't you want to know what he said?"

"Yes. But first I want to hear about the contract before my mother gets back and derails the conversation."

"Hmm. And she is in rare form today, let me tell you!"

"Now *I'm* sorry," he said.

"Please. It's not your fault. She's worried about you. That's all."

"So, what about Agnes?"

"She's looked over the contract."

"And?"

"It's better than I expected. Frankly, more than I figured I was worth."

"See. What did I tell you? Never underestimate yourself."

She squeezed his hand.

"Oh, good. They're here to poke and prod me again," he said, nodding at the nurse who'd just entered. "Why don't you go and grab some tea or something."

Lily hesitated.

"Go on," he said, grinning. "I promise I'm not going anywhere."

"Ok," she said. She stood, and then leaned over the bed to give him a quick kiss.

Only after she'd left the room did he allow his smile to fade.

Several hours into their vigil, after Maggie had shifted and plumped his pillow for the umpteenth time that day, Tony had finally had enough.

"Mum, it's fine. Really. Leave it."

"Well, I thought that—"

"Mum, enough. Please."

He looked over at Lily, and then turned to his sister for assistance. "Do you think perhaps Lily and I might have another moment?"

Anna smiled. "Mum, why don't we pop round to the cafeteria for a cuppa?"

Maggie, frowning, reluctantly followed Anna out of the room.

Once they'd gone, Tony turned to Lily, who was sitting with her tablet on her lap, staring out the window.

"Lil?"

She brightened at the sound of his voice, and he wiggled his finger for her to join him.

She set the tablet on the sofa and moved toward his bed. "Hiya," she said. She ran her fingers through his hair and tucked a few strands behind one ear.

He grasped her wrist. "Are you okay?"

"Yeah. Sure. I'm just trying to stay out of your mother's way," she laughed.

"You've been awfully quiet."

"I'm fine. I'm just…"

"Tired?"

"A little," she admitted.

"Worrying?"

"A little," she said again with a light laugh.

"Don't."

"I'm trying," she said.

"Just think, a week from now all of this will nearly be a memory."

"I hope you're right," she said.

He regarded her for a moment then said, "You should probably go back to the hotel and get some rest."

She tipped her head. "What?"

"I'll be fine here," he said.

"I'm sure you will, but—"

"Of course I will. You should go."

"You really want me to leave?" she asked.

"Not exactly," he said, "but I need you to go. I need to know that you're taking care of yourself. And..."

"Yes?"

He paused and looked toward the door to verify they were still alone, "I need you to go... so you can take my mother with you!"

Lily laughed. "Ah ha!"

"Please, Lil!" he pleaded. "She's making me crazy."

"It's only been a few hours."

"You didn't hear her. She's talking about sleeping here tonight. You have to get her out of here."

"She means well."

"I know that. And I love her. But I don't need my mummy to spend the night with me."

"I thought I might spend the night with you."

"*You...* might be a different story," he said with a lilt of longing in his voice. "Still, I could use some time... *without* an audience."

She said nothing, but her eyes begged, "Please don't make me go."

"Please, Lil." He cupped her cheek in his hand and gently ran a thumb over her bottom lip, freeing it from her teeth.

She made herself smile at him again, reading the irritation in his eyes. He had always been the strong one, the healthy one. He was the protector. This role reversal was new and unwelcome. But if it was time he needed, she would give it to him. Even if it broke her heart to leave him.

"Okay." She began to pack up her tablet and things. "Well, I guess I'll see you in the morning?"

"I have a better idea. When you get Mum and Anna settled, go down to the hotel bar. Have a drink. Hell, have one for each of us. Then go back up to the room and call me."

"Are you sure you're not too tired?"

"I was only pretending to be asleep earlier so Mum would leave me alone for five minutes."

She laughed.

"Anyway, I want your voice to be the last thing I hear before I go to sleep tonight."

It would be, she thought, if you'd let me stay. But she knew he needed space. "Talk to you later, then," she said as she leaned over and kissed him.

"Oh, right! Now we know why he wanted us to leave," Anna joked as they came back in with to-go cups in their hands.

"You caught me," Tony said with a forced smile. "No, actually, we were just saying goodnight, weren't we, love?"

"Yes, we were. And you two have had a terribly long day. Are you ready to go?" Lily asked Anna.

"Oh, yes. I suppose so," Anna said.

Maggie looked horrified at the suggestion.

"Come on Maggie," Lily said, patting her back. "Tuck him in and kiss him goodnight. Let's let him get some rest, hmm?"

Maggie looked at Lily and Anna and then back at Tony.

"I'll be fine, Mum," he assured her.

"We'll be back first thing in the morning," Lily said. She opened the door and stood waiting for the others to exit.

"Fine. Anna, remind me to call Grace in the morning and give her an update," Maggie said as she left.

Lily rolled her eyes at the mention of Tony's former fiancée. She turned to him. "Call me if you need anything at all?"

"I will," he promised.

She whispered, "Je t'aime," as she blew him kiss.

He caught it and held it to his heart as he always did. "Thank you," he mouthed.

He waited until they were all safely down the hall before attempting to shift positions. If any one of them heard even the slightest groan or caught him grimacing in pain, he would never be rid of them.

12
LUCKY BREAK

The next few days passed slowly with Tony still resisting attention from all of the women in his life. Fortunately, what remained of his left kidney seemed to be keeping up with its end of the deal, and the fact that all of the known cancer had been removed made Tony hopeful and allowed Lily and the others to relax somewhat.

By the end of the following week, Anna was able to turn her attention back to her law practice and the fact that she had a custody hearing due to be heard in a few days. With some effort, she managed to convince Maggie that Tony was out of the woods and it was safe to return to London. Maggie hesitantly booked their flight for that Sunday.

On Friday evening when Anna and Maggie left the hospital to pack, Lily and Tony both breathed a sigh of relief, happy to finally have a moment alone to just *be*.

While Tony dozed quietly, Lily curled up in the recliner next to his bed. She had just about fallen asleep herself when her phone vibrated with a text message.

- **Lillian, are you really still in LA?**

Javier Martinez. They'd worked together on the set of *Last Dance* years ago and occasionally since. She pursed her lips, wondering what he might want. She answered.

- **Yes, Javi. Why?**
- Fabulous! Heard the news?
- **Been busy. What news?**
- Lisette Garcia was arrested last night.
- **What happened?**
- Nailed after too many shots of tequila.
- **Oh no!**
- Right?! Never fuck with a Malibu mailbox.
- **Did she hit one?**
- Three of them.
- **Shit!**
- I know, right? Eduardo is fucking pissed. He's going to have her little Latina ass fired. In the middle of production!!!

Lily chuckled. She could just imagine Javier's flamboyant stance and thick Venezuelan accent as she read the words.

Tony stirred when she laughed and Lily looked up. Once he'd settled again, she went back to texting.

- **Fired for hitting a mailbox? She's gotten away with worse.**
- One of them was Eduardo's!!!
- **Oh! Faux pas.**
- Exactly! So... he needs a new partner for the video.
- **Who are they looking at?**
- You!!! Didn't your agent tell you?
- **Ha ha!**
- No joke. Showed him the Skyfall video.
- **He liked it?**
- Loved it!
- **But Lisette is ten years younger and Columbian.**
- She's also 10x more bitchy!
- **LOL. You have a point.**
- Of course I do. Besides, dark hair, gorgeous body. Once they dim the lights and spray on the tan, it won't matter, honey.

Lily couldn't help but laugh again.

"What's so funny?" Tony said groggily.

"Sorry, sweetheart. I didn't mean to wake you. I just had a funny text," Lily said.

He stretched cautiously without asking from whom. But as Lily fired text after text, he began to wonder. He found himself hoping it wasn't Charles, though there was no real reason to assume it was.

A few minutes later she volunteered, "Have I ever talked to you about Javier Martinez?"

"He played Marco in the movie."

"Yep. Well, he's working on the new Eduardo Mendoza video and—"

"As in *the* Eduardo Mendoza? The Latin heart-throb?"

"Yes! And, long story short, they need someone to step in and dance with him."

"And they want you?"

"They want me!" She lit up.

"That's fantastic," Tony said. Then he watched her smile fade. "What?" he said.

"It is great. You know, it's great to know they wanted me."

"But?"

She shrugged. "If the circumstances were different—"

"Lily..."

"They're filming on Wednesday, so..."

"So what's the problem?"

"You're only going to be released tomorrow. It would be two full days including rehearsals. I don't want to leave you alone so soon. Not for that long.

"I'll be fine."

"You might be. But I would worry."

"Is that all that's stopping you?"

She shrugged again.

He thought for a moment then said, "I'm certain we could persuade my mother to stay a little longer."

"Really?" she said. "You would agree to that?"

"I'm not thrilled about the idea, but if it would make you feel better..."

"It would. A little. But—"

"Lily," he groaned.

She joined him on the bed. "Darling, I don't want to ask her to do that. Look, I already told him I couldn't do it. So—"

"Are you crazy? You'd better call him and fix it before they find someone else. Lily, this is huge."

"I know that! But—"

"Call him. Please. Don't let my situation keep you from doing this."

"It's not only that, you know?"

"What then?"

She frowned. "It would be a lot of work in a very short period of time. I've seen the kinds of things that Javi puts together these days. It would be... a lot. Some of the lifts he uses... And Eduardo is so high-energy."

"You'll be fine."

She noted the assumptive tone, as if he expected her to do it. "Probably," she said. "But I'd only have two days. I'm not sure it'll be enough."

"Hmm. Not only that, but you're used to giving direction on the dance floor, not taking it." He laughed.

"Ha! That too."

He rubbed her hand reassuringly. "You'll be fabulous."

She smiled. He could tell she was considering the idea, weighing the risks.

"Come on, love. Go for it," he said. "You've gotta risk it to get the biscuit!" he added with a wink.

She laughed. "Okay. I'll make you a deal. I'll talk to Javi about the situation. Depending on how things go…"

"I'm telling you, it'll be fine! I don't want you to miss this."

She bit her lip for a few seconds before another smile snuck across her face. "I'll see what we can work out."

13
JUST TURKEY

Tony was released the next day with extensive instructions on dressings, meds, diet and exercise. He was thrilled to be escaping the white, sterile, watchful environment of the hospital, though he was hardly looking forward to being under the watchful eye of one woman or another once he was back in the hotel.

Lily was happy to be taking him home, if one could call a hotel home, but she was nervous too. Patience was not among Tony's virtues, and he hated to be limited. She worried that he would attempt too much too soon. She worried that he wouldn't be forthcoming with his symptoms, trying to be too strong. And she worried about having his mother to contend with.

Maggie had taken little convincing. In fact, she seemed almost happy to have a reason to stay, if only for a few more days. But while her attitude toward Lily had improved, it was still far from welcoming. Lily feared what might happen without Anna there to run interference.

Maggie arrived bright and early on Tuesday morning to take her shift as head nurse.

Lily wished Tony luck and, after a quick kiss and a bit more reassuring that he really did want her to go, she set off for her day of rehearsal.

* * *

When the crew finally broke for lunch, Lily sat down in a quiet corner to view the footage she'd asked one of the assistants to record with her cell phone. It was rudimentary, but it would be enough for her to see what needed improvement. She watched it once and started it over.

"Aren't you going to eat?"

Lily looked up. "Charles? What the hell are you doing here?"

"I was in the neighborhood and I thought I'd come by and see how you were doing."

"How did you know I was here?"

"I asked James."

"Oh. Right. Thank you, by the way. For letting me... have his services?"

"No problem."

She continued to fiddle with her phone.

He looked around for a bit before continuing. "So, how's it going?"

She sighed. "It's going okay. I think we're making pretty good progress."

"That's good. But that's not what I meant."

"Oh, me? I'm fine." She shrugged and put the phone down long enough to tighten her ponytail. "Tony is resting comfortably. For now."

"And you're trying not to worry about the fact that you're here instead of there with him."

She sighed. "Yes. It helps to keep busy, though," she said. She picked the phone up again and stared at a new text message. "Maggie says he's doing fine."

"Well, then, why don't you let me take you to lunch."

"Thanks, but I think I'll probably just go down to the coffee shop."

"Come on. That's not going to be enough. You need energy for this afternoon."

She fiddled with a piece of stray hair and bit her lip. "I should call him, just to be sure," she said.

"Tony would want you to eat," Charles pointed out.

She pursed her lips, knowing he was right. Her expression gave him hope.

He held out his hand. "We can hit that sandwich place you like on the Boulevard. And... I brought the Ferrari," he said with a cavalier smile, his out-stretched hand still hovering above her.

She shook her head in defeat. "Fine." She reached for his hand, but pulled herself up from her cross-legged position with very little help from him.

"You never could resist a rich man in a fast car," he joked.

"Ha! More like I can't resist a turkey, bacon, and avocado."

"Yeah. That's just as good," he said. "Is your back bothering you?" he asked when she winced.

"It's fine."

"Lil…" he said. His tone sounded like a fatherly warning.

She rolled her eyes. "If you must know, it's killing me."

"When's the last time you had an adjustment?"

"It'll be fine. Javier and Eduardo are kicking my ass right now," she said. "And…" She leaned into him and whispered, "Don't tell anyone, but I may be getting too old for this."

"Never! When's the last time you had an adjustment?" he asked again.

"Not that long ago."

"When?"

"Charles!" she groaned.

"When?" he asked again.

"Before we left New York," she admitted.

"You should call Doctor McGraw's office. I'm sure they could get you in."

"I will when I get a chance, all right? I don't know if you've noticed, but I'm a bit busy at the moment."

"You need to take care of yourself, Lil."

"Oh, good Lord! Have you been talking to Tony? Come on. I've only got an hour," she said, hustling him toward the exit.

* * *

They cruised out of the parking lot in the cherry-red Ferrari California, top down, pausing only briefly at the exit for the security guard to greet Charles. As they pulled through the gate, Charles looked over at Lily. She was leaning back on the seat with her eyes closed. The late morning sun lit her face and a light breeze blew the wisps that had escaped her ponytail.

"Nice day," he said.

"Mmm. It's beautiful," she said. She sat up and stretched.

He watched her arch her back and extend her long, gorgeous neck. *You're beautiful. Fucking hot, actually,* he thought. But he didn't say it. He said nothing. Neither of them did. So, he turned on some music to fill the silence.

Lily immediately started to laugh. "Please tell me this is the radio and not a playlist."

"Why?"

"'We Built This City?'"

"What about it?"

"It's only the most repetitive, un-danceable song ever!"

"Hey, I've known plenty of women who like that song," he said, trying to sound suave.

"Yeah? When? In the eighties?" she chided.

121

"Well, excuse me!" He smirked, pretending to be annoyed. Truthfully, he found her outspoken side very attractive. He skipped to the next song.

Lily recognized "Back in Black" the moment she heard the opening drum sequence. She tried to ignore the images of Tony that immediately sprang to mind, but she could feel a slow heat spreading through her entire body. She reached for the button to skip it.

"That's a classic. What could you possibly have against that one?" Charles said.

"Nothing. I have nothing against it. I just... Oh good Lord!"

"TNT" blared through the speakers and she reached for the skip button again. This time he swatted her hand away.

"Why do you hate AC/DC all of a sudden?"

"I don't," she said, shaking her head. "I'm just not... in the mood... for AC/DC," she said.

He pulled up at a stop light and looked over at her. Her face was all rosy. She shifted slightly in her seat and he had a flashback to her similarly awkward behavior during the love scenes at the screening of *Jillian Jones.*

"Oh my God!" he said in disturbed amusement. "Don't tell me..."

"What?"

"Don't tell me this is your sexy song!"

"What?"

"Your music to fuck by."

"Oh, please!" she said, trying to fake shock.

"That's great! Just what I need! A visual of you two banging to AC/DC."

"Stop! We do not!" she said, but her face was even redder than before.

He laughed as he skipped to the next song. "Is Aerosmith acceptable? Or do you do it to that, too?"

She looked away and mumbled something.

"What?" he pushed her.

"Fine! Just... It's fine," she said.

Steven Tyler did all of the talking for the remainder of the ride. Lily was too embarrassed to say anything else. Charles was too busy removing Tony from the sex scenes playing in his head and putting himself in his place, imagining all of the things he'd like to do to her. All the things he'd love for her to do to him.

By the time they got their sandwiches, Charles had moved on to talking about an upcoming project.

After lunch, Lily thanked him for the meal and the distraction and went back to work.

Charles watched her walk away, wondering just how far he'd have to go to become more than just a distraction.

* * *

When they wrapped up for the day, it was after nine. Lily was exhausted. She couldn't wait to get back to the hotel, almost as anxious to get to sleep as she was to see Tony.

After dismissing Maggie, she snuck into the bedroom and found Tony asleep with a *Men's Health* magazine open on his chest. She sat on the edge of the bed, carefully slid the magazine from his chest, and peeked at it to see what he'd been reading. She felt a pang in her chest as she read the title: "Ten Foods to Fight Cancer." She closed it with a quiet sigh and laid it on the bedside table. She watched him for a few minutes then forced herself to stand up. She began peeling off her workout clothes as she walked into the master bath. After a quick shower, she brushed her teeth and put on a pair of shorty pajamas. She turned out the light and crawled carefully into bed next to him.

He stirred and turned onto his side with his back toward her.

Lily moved as close to him as she dared, not wanting to wake him or put any unnecessary pressure on his incisions. In the moonlit room she watched the rise and fall of his silhouette. His breath sounded a little ragged in the stillness. She gently slipped her arm around him, avoiding the bandages on his midsection.

Tony's fingers folded around hers at once and his breathing returned to a slower, steadier rhythm.

Lily smiled in the darkness. Even in his sleep, his body responded to hers, she thought. Comforted by the thought and grounded for the first time since she'd left him that morning, she drifted off to sleep.

* * *

The next day she was in hair and make-up by seven a.m., looking forward to a brutal shooting schedule.

"Keep your head up, please," the stylist kept saying as Lily texted Tony for the third time.

"Sorry," Lily said, but she finished the message and sent it anyway. She knew she'd have little chance to do so the rest of the day.

She was thrilled when they wrapped up at eight-thirty that evening. She quickly changed into her street clothes and headed for the door, still in full makeup.

* * *

"Hello," she called as she opened the door to the suite. No answer.

The room was dark except for the soft glow from the television coming through the crack in the bedroom door. She dropped her dance bag on the floor and stowed her coat in the closet. She chuckled as she approached the bedroom, realizing that he was watching another episode of *House Hunters International.* He loved that show. She, on the other hand, found most of the couples annoying.

She pushed the door open and found him sleeping again. Her heart sank. She crept over to the bed and placed a wisp of a kiss on his forehead.

"Hello, angel," he said before he'd even opened his eyes.

She jumped, but her face immediately lit up. "I thought you were asleep," she said.

"I was just resting my eyes. Waiting for you," he said, blinking. He eyed her, still surprised by the sight of her in stage make-up. He ought to have been used to it by now, but the heavy eyeliner and lipstick always caught him a little off guard. He much preferred her usual look. It was softer, more subdued, allowing her natural beauty to shine through.

"How was your day?" she asked, perching on the edge of the bed.

"It was fine," he said. He rubbed his eyes. "We had tea. We went for a bit of a walk out by the pool."

"That's nice."

"Yes. And then I attempted to answer emails while Mum worked on one of her crossword puzzles."

Lily laughed ruefully, imagining how terribly bored he must have been. "I'm sorry," she said.

"It was fine. Really. But I *did* miss you." He grasped the back of her neck and pulled her down toward him so that he could kiss her.

"Mmm," Lily purred happily. Her eyes remained closed for a second as she savored the kiss. "So, how did you get rid of her?"

"Ha! I convinced her to finish packing up and get some sleep. Dad will be here tomorrow afternoon."

"It's awfully nice of him to fly all the way over just to pick her up."

"Yes, well, she hates to fly alone. Besides, I think he was glad for the excuse to come and see us. Never mind all of that," he said, quickly changing course. "What about you?" he asked. "How did it go today?" he asked as he turned off the television and carefully leaned over to turn on the light.

"It went well, I think."

Judging by the twinkle in her eyes, he guessed she was down-playing her excitement for his benefit. As if she felt guilty.

"That's it? Just well?"

She smiled then and stood, throwing her arms in the air. "Eduardo was amazing! And the choreography... Wait 'til you see it!"

"That's wonderful," he said.

"Yes," she said, reeling in her excitement again. "But I'm glad it's over. It feels like I haven't had time to breathe."

She sat on the ottoman across the room and slipped off her ballet flats. She crossed one ankle over the other knee and began to crack her toes.

"Let's have them," he said, gesturing toward her feet. He wiggled and flexed his fingers in preparation.

She pried herself off of the stool and sat at the foot of the bed again. He tossed a pillow at her and she leaned on it against the foot of the bed with her legs stretched out next to him. He took the left foot into his lap and began to massage it.

"Mmm. You are a magician," she murmured.

"If only I could show you the rest of my tricks," he teased.

She winked at him as she skimmed her bottom lip with her teeth. "Soon, darling. Soon." She closed her eyes and laid back. "As exhilarating as it was, I may have to consider hanging up my dance shoes."

"Not on my account."

"No. I've just never felt so worn out in all my life."

"Stress, love. It takes a lot out of a person."

"I suppose you're right," she said sleepily.

"I know I am," he said.

She wanted to give him an endearing look, but without the strength to open her eyes, the only thing she could offer was a slight curl of her lips.

"Have you eaten?" he asked as he moved on to her other foot.

"Ha!"

"What?"

"Nothing. It's just that Charles came by to take me to lunch yesterday and..." She let the thought go thinking Tony probably wouldn't enjoy being compared to Charles, no matter what the context.

"You had lunch with him?" he said, his fingers still.

"Mmm hmm," she said nonchalantly.

His face was suddenly serious.

"It was a turkey sandwich, darling," she assured him. "Nothing more."

He exhaled. "Of course not. I didn't mean to assume..." he said, looking down. His fingers resumed their work.

"Well, there was a bit more," she admitted.

"Like what?" he asked cautiously.

She pulled her foot free and stood. She paced for a moment then sat next to him again. "Bacon," she said with as straight a face as she could muster.

At that, Tony nearly burst out laughing, but resisted, acting horrified. "You shared bacon with Charles!" he said with exaggerated surprise.

"I didn't say that!" she laughed. "We did not share."

"You didn't?" he said. He looked deep into her eyes, trying to carry off the concerned act.

"No. I swear," she said, pretending to be equally serious. "I will never again share Charles George's bacon."

"Never?"

"Not as long as I live," she said.

"All right, then. No bacon." He pulled her down toward him.

She braced herself to keep from putting all of her weight on him. "Nope."

"And no bangers and mash," he said, no longer able to contain his laughter.

"Ha! No. I promise you... I will never have bangers and mash with another man." She kissed him quick on the lips to seal the deal and stood up again.

He looked happy, she thought, as she admired his smile. "I'm just gonna get a shower before I pass out," she said.

He watched her walk slowly, gingerly into the en suite. He could tell how tired and sore she was. A month ago he would have escorted her into the shower. He'd have lathered and rinsed her. And after toweling her off, he'd have carried her to bed and massaged every inch of her naked body until it no longer ached, or until the ache was no longer the painful kind.

Now, however, he was too tired to get out of bed. He leaned back and listened. He could just make out the sound of Lily singing the new Eduardo Mendoza song over the hum of the shower. Tired as she was, he thought, she was still vibrant and beautiful.

He closed his eyes and hoped his fatigue would subside soon. He wanted to believe it would, that it was just the after effects of multiple surgeries, as Lily kept assuring him. But he couldn't help but wonder... what if?

A few minutes later he heard the *Peanuts* theme playing in the bathroom. "Charles," Tony sighed. He listened. The shower stopped almost immediately and he heard Lily answer the phone. She sounded positively perky as she chatted to him about her day.

What if... he thought again. What if his strength didn't return? What if he didn't get better? What if he didn't have enough life left in him to keep up with her? Where would that leave them?

14
STRIKE THREE

Lily's phone vibrated on the nightstand, rousing her from sleep. She grabbed for it, squinting in the morning sunlight. Nine a.m. and already four missed calls from Agnes. She groaned and made herself sit up. Her hand immediately clutched at the back of her head as pain spread across the base of her skull. She took a breath and proceeded to type a one-handed text.

- **Morning, Aggy. What's up?**
- Afternoon, Lil. ☺ Big news. Meeting in five. IM me.

She smiled in spite of pain and eased back down onto the pillow. She gave herself five minutes then told herself to suck it up and climbed out of bed.

Tony awoke a while later. He turned toward Lily's side of the bed. It was empty. He couldn't remember when she came to bed the night before. Charles. She'd been on the phone with Charles. How long had that lasted, he wondered. He looked at the clock. He'd slept for more than ten hours, but he still felt tired. He eased himself out of bed and made his way to the bathroom, finding himself irritated that even the morning trip to the toilet could feel like so much work.

He made it out of the bedroom and found Lily on the sofa with her laptop, busily click-clacking away.

"Good morning, glory," she said with a bright smile.

He forced himself to return her smile. "Watcha working on?" he asked as he approached her.

"Just messaging Agnes." She tilted her head, exposing her cheek for him to kiss it.

The computer dinged and she began to type furiously again. "Are you hungry? Breakfast'll be here in any minute," she said without waiting for an answer.

As if on cue, there was a knock at the door, "Shall I get that?" he asked.

"No. Sit! I've got it," she said. She sprang from the couch.

He moved slowly to the small table at the other side of the room as the server wheeled the cart of food into the room.

Once plates of scrambled eggs and fruit had been unloaded, the young woman handed Lily the check presenter. She watched Lily intently, glancing down as Lily signed her name. "Oh my God, you *are* her," she twittered, her cheeks suddenly pink. "Sorry," she added shyly. But her commentary didn't stop. "Oh my... You're really *the* Lily Josephson?"

"Yes," Lily admitted.

"Oh my God!" the woman squealed. "*Last Dance* was only the best movie ever! I am like a total fangirl! Seriously!"

"Oh, thank you," Lily said with a chuckle.

"Do you think there will be a fifteenth anniversary special? It's coming up, isn't it?"

Lily shook her head. "I couldn't say. We'll have to wait and see about that."

"It's so nice meet you!"

"Likewise," Lily said, as she began to gently usher her toward the door. "Always nice to meet a fan."

Tony chuckled as she closed the door.

"Can you believe that?" Lily said. "She must be new. I've never had the staff react that way in a hotel of this caliber."

"Hmm," Tony said. He glanced at her over his cup of coffee. "Is there an actual possibility of an anniversary special?" he asked.

She nibbled her lip, looking like the cat who ate the canary. "Well, Charles mentioned the possibility a few weeks ago."

"You gave her the standard *no comment* answer just now. Have you heard something?"

"Actually," she smiled, "that's what Agnes and I were just messaging about. It's a go!"

"Congratulations," he said. "That's great news."

"Isn't it? She's firming up the details now."

"Who?"

"Agnes."

"Oh."

"And Mason says—"

"Who?"

"Ken Mason."

"Who's that?"

"The director. You remember? You used to call him Malibu Ken."

He looked at her curiously.

"Of *Last Dance*," she said.

"Right."

"He wants to set up a meeting with me about choreographing an ensemble number for the cast!"

"When?"

"I don't know. Soon."

"This has been quite the productive trip for you," he said.

"It really has!" she said as she piled all but one of her pieces of dry toast on his plate.

She perched on her chair with her knees pulled up to her chest and popped a strawberry into her mouth. She observed him as she chewed. He seemed happy for her. At least his words said as much, but he didn't look it.

He smiled again when he noticed her scrutinizing him and took a bite of toast, hoping that would disguise his agitation and buy him a few moments of silence to gather his wits about him.

It didn't.

"Are you all right?" she asked as she stabbed a piece of melon.

"Just tired this morning is all," he said.

"I know the feeling," she said. She heard the ding of another message and unfolded herself to go answer it.

They ate the rest of their breakfast without much talk. Or at least he ate. She managed only a few more bites of fruit and a nibble of her remaining slice of bread.

"Aren't you going to eat those?" he asked, pointing at her eggs.

She shook her head. "I guess I wasn't as hungry as I thought," she said. Her head was still throbbing. She picked up her phone. "Do you think you'll be okay for a bit if I go out?"

"Where are you going?"

"Dr. McGraw. My chiropractor. I can call your mum if—"

"No. You won't be long. I'll be fine." He picked up his phone too. "Fuck!" he said.

"What?"

"Is it really Thursday?"

"Yes."

"Shit! I completely missed the conference call with Sam and Nigel."

"I'm sure Sam handled it," she said.

"I'm sure he did, but I told him I would call. What time is it in London? Lily? What time is it in London?"

"Oh," she said, surprised he actually needed to ask. "Ah... ten... one... six."

"Six. Okay. I'm gonna go call him now," he said.

She moved to help him get up from the table as he made a second attempt to stand.

"I've got it!" he snapped. "I'm fine."

Once he'd closed the bedroom door she let out a sigh. She took a long sip of coffee and dialed Dr. McGraw's office.

Freshly adjusted and massaged, Lily put her things away and went to check on Tony. He was asleep again, his laptop and phone on the bed next to him.

She sat. "Hey you," she said softly, her hand resting on his chest.

"Mmm. Hi. How are you?"

"I was just going to ask you the same thing."

"I'm all right. Not very productive today, but all right."

"I brought you some lunch. Nothing exciting. Just a sandwich and some soup."

"Hmm. I don't need an exciting lunch. You're exciting enough," he said with a sleepy smile. His hand slipped up under the hem of her skirt as he caressed her thigh.

She took his hand in hers. "Ha! Okay. Would you like me to bring it in here or would you rather have it out there?"

"I'll come out there. Just give me a minute."

"Take your time," she said. She leaned over and kissed him.

She set his lunch out and took a bottle of water from the mini fridge. She checked her email and sent a text to her brother. When Tony still hadn't emerged, she decided to check on him once more.

She peeked in the door. He was sitting up on the edge of the bed in his robe. "I thought maybe you'd fallen asleep again," she joked.

"No. Just can't seem get started today."

She crossed the room and stopped short when she reached him. Without a word, she went to the dresser and pulled out a pair of athletic pants and a clean T-shirt for him.

"What are you doing?" he asked as she tossed them down next to him.

"I'm gonna help you get dressed."

"Why?"

"Because we need to get you back to hospital."

* * *

"The confusion, the swelling, the fatigue... They're all classic symptoms of acute renal failure," the nephrologist said.

"I thought he was recovering." Lily said. Why is this happening?"

"I don't know the exact cause right now. We'll need to run a few tests. The only thing we know for sure is that the kidney he has left is no longer keeping up with its end of the bargain."

Lily and Tony exchanged a silent glance.

"The kidney is failing?" Tony asked, needing further confirmation.

"Yes."

"Can you fix it?" Lily asked.

"I don't know at the moment. I don't know if it's going to be a chronic problem or not, but we have to do the job for it until we can figure out what's going on."

Lily reached for Tony's hand.

"I'm going to put in an order for a neckline and we'll get the process started." The doctor gave a half-smile and hurried out of the room.

"Dialysis," Tony sighed.

Lily looked at him, speechless. She didn't need to speak. Her teary eyes said everything.

"Well, at least that explains why I've been so bloody exhausted today, hmm?"

She didn't respond.

He squeezed her hand.

Minutes later the doctor returned with a nurse and Lily stepped out into the hallway to make room for them and their equipment. She checked the time, wondering if she should call Maggie. Tony would likely ask her not to, but if she didn't, Maggie would never let her hear the end of it.

She dialed. No answer. She took a breath as she waited for the beep. "Hi, Maggie. It's Lily. You're probably at the airport waiting for Joe's flight. Just... Call me when you get this, okay? Bye."

She hung up and texted Danny, sniffing to keep from breaking down.

- **Are u busy?**
- Always. LOL. Just catching an early dinner with the fam before curtain.
- **Have a good show. Call me later pls.**
- Sure. Everything ok?

Not wanting to disrupt Danny's dinner, she put her phone in her pocket without answering. She fell back against the wall and looked up. Realistically, she knew dialysis wasn't the end of the world, but it seemed as though Tony had suffered one stroke of bad luck after another and she couldn't help but fear the worst. Tears in her eyes, she started her silent prayer.

"Dear God, please don't take him from me. Not now. Please."

When the phone rang a moment later, she stifled her tears and took a couple of deep breaths. One hand on her stomach to suppress the nausea, she pulled the phone from her pocket. "Hi," she answered, expecting it to be Danny.

"Hey, Lil."

"Oh, Charles. Hello," she said, trying to sound in control.

"I just ran into Ken Mason. He said you guys are in talks."

"Yes, we are. Charles, could I call you back, please?"

"No need, really. I just wanted to congratulate you. Is something wrong?"

"I'm sorry," she sniffed. "I can't do this right now." She stopped talking just to keep from sobbing and hung up.

He called back immediately, but she ignored the call.

By the time Maggie and Joe arrived at the hospital, the catheter was in place and the dialysis was in progress. Maggie gasped when she pushed open the door and saw Tony lying flat on his back as tubes, red with blood, connected him to the machine.

Lily looked up from her place at Tony's bedside. She kissed the back of his hand and laid it gently at his side. She stood ran her fingers through his hair.

"Your parents are here," she whispered. "I'll give you a minute."

"You don't have to go."

"I'll be back," she assured him as she kissed his forehead. She nodded to Maggie and smiled at Joe as she stepped out. "I'm glad you made it safely."

Joe stopped her just long enough to give her a quick peck on the cheek, and then went to his son.

"Hey champ," she heard him say as she closed the door. She felt a slight pain in her chest.

15
FAMILY MATTERS

Maggie and Joe appeared at the doorway of the small waiting area a while later.

Lily looked up from her conversation with Danny. "I'll have to let you go, sweetie," she said.

She hung up the phone and watched them as they walked silently into the room hand in hand. They sat facing her, both polished and put together, but looking somber. It was surreal, she thought. Like a scene from a movie. With a British Helen Mirren and Hugh Grant's father. She chuckled inwardly at her own wandering thoughts and coughed to cover it up. Maggie would be appalled to know she'd found even the slightest bit of humor in the whole situation. "How is he?" she asked.

Maggie blinked and pressed her lips together.

"He's holding up as well as can be expected," Joe said. "I expect he'll sleep for a while after it's finished."

Lily nodded.

"Have they told you any more about his condition... in the long term?" Joe asked.

"Not much," Lily said. "They believe they got all of the cancer. But the kidney... No. They don't know yet if or when it will recover."

"So the dialysis... it could be..."

Lily swallowed. "Permanent. Yes."

Maggie reached for Joe's hand again.

"Have the two of you talked about what you'll do if it is... permanent?" Joe asked.

"Not really," Lily said. "I think he just wanted to believe it wouldn't be an issue and I didn't push him. I guess I thought it was better to be positive."

"Of course," Joe agreed.

"Not very practical though, is it?" Lily said. She stood and walked toward the coffee machine in the corner. She poured herself a cup, more for something to do than out of desire to drink it. She held up the pot and motioned to Maggie and Joe. "Coffee?"

"No, thank you," Joe said.

Lily took a sip from her cup. No Starbucks, she thought. She noticed Maggie eyeing Joe expectantly, but he'd fallen silent.

"What is it?" she asked, taking a seat across from them again.

Joe shook his head.

Maggie cleared her throat and spoke. "We were thinking... if the situation doesn't improve... it might be best for him to be around family. That way he'll have people

143

around who can look after him. I mean, on a regular basis."

"What are you saying?" Lily asked, the knot in her stomach beginning to tighten.

"I'm saying we'd—"

"Not we," Margaret," Joe said under his breath.

"Fine. I. I'd like to take him home to London with us."

Heat immediately filled Lily's face as bile and fury created an unpleasant mix in the pit of her stomach. "Is that what he told you he wants?" she asked.

"Not exactly, but—"

"He's not twelve, you know? You can't just make that decision for him," Lily said.

"I'll talk to him, of course, but I just think it would be best for him to be around friends and family."

"He has friends. *We* have friends at home in New York."

"Of course you do, but we're his family. We can take care of him."

Lily shook her head. Her lip quivered. "You're his family."

"Yes."

"And what am I? Hmm? Or doesn't that matter?"

"Of course it matters, but... You're busy. You're working. He may need someone to..."

"To do what? Watch over him twenty-four hours a day, like he's a time bomb waiting to explode? He'd hate that and you know it!" She strode toward the door, propelled by her anger.

"Lily, wait. We haven't finished—"

"Oh, yes we 'ave."

"Where are you going?"

"I'm going back to sit with 'im. Get my time in while I 'ave the chance."

"Well, that went well," Joe said when Lily had gone. Lily was obviously upset. Her Cockney had come out.

"You were a lot of help. Thank you very much," Maggie said.

"What did you want me to say?"

"You could have backed me up."

"Did you really expect me to agree with you?"

"Yes."

"Why? She's right, Mags. He's a big boy. He needs to make his own decisions, live his own life, whatever that means. And she's part of that life. You can't just ignore that."

"I'm not. I just think—"

"You just think you can take better care of him than she can. I know. But the thing is... he doesn't want you to."

Maggie scowled, but had no response.

"Come on," he said, putting his arm around her. "Let's go back to the hotel. Maybe get a bite to eat."

"We should say good-bye to him, don't you think?" she said pitifully.

"We said good night earlier. Let him rest. Let her stay with him. We'll come back first thing tomorrow morning."

"What if something happens and we're not here?"

"Lily's here," he reminded her. "The doctors are keeping a close eye on him." He squeezed her tighter and kissed her hair. "It'll be all right, my love."

"How can you know that?" she said.

"I don't know it. But I have to have faith. *We* have to have faith. For his sake."

16
FOR PITY'S SAKE

Even after the dialysis was finished Tony was exhausted. Lily got him into a pair of pajamas and helped him back into bed.

He sighed as she tucked the covers up around him. "I hate that you have to see me like this," he said.

"Like what? I've seen you in your pajamas plenty of times," she said, her lips curling slightly. "Of course, I've also seen you out of them," she said with a tiny sparkle in her eye.

"You know what I mean."

"Tomorrow will be better," she promised, folding his robe and straightening his slippers at the end of his bed.

"So they tell me," he said. "Until they need to do it again."

Lily swallowed, choking a bit on that thought, but she forced herself to keep smiling at him. She wanted to remain hopeful. She wanted him to remain hopeful. Her attempted cover didn't fool him.

The look on her face, a cross between pity and grief, cut like a knife. Whether it did more damage to his heart or his pride, he couldn't say. He'd always been the strong one. He'd been the one to comfort her after the brutal fights with her father. He'd dried her tears for years on the anniversary of her mother's death. She'd told him countless times that he gave her strength. But now, he had no way to ease her pain. Worse, he was the cause of it.

"You've been crying again," he said.

She nodded. No point in trying to deny it. She walked around the bed and paused in front of the window.

Tony watched her, searching for something to say that might make her feel better, but he came up with nothing. "I'm sorry," he said. And he *was* sorry. For the twelve years they'd spent apart. The wasted time. Sorry for what his illness was putting her through. Sorry for himself.

"Don't apologize," she said. "It's not your fault."

"I just hate what this is doing—"

"It's not the cancer," she said. "Your mother thinks you should go home with her. To London."

"I take it you aren't a fan of the idea."

"Are you?" she asked. She'd expected him to be immediately outraged as she'd been.

"Of going with my mother? No, but—" He read the anguish on her face. "Lil, we've talked about this before. I would love to live in England on a more permanent basis. You know that."

Lily seemed to consider the idea, but after a minute she shook her head sadly. "I can't, Tony. I just can't. With all of the opportunities that have come up here..."

"You're not going to suggest we stay here in California, are you?"

"No! I wouldn't do that to you. But commuting from New York to L.A. is do-able. London to L.A.... And what about Josie? I know she's not mine. I do. But I couldn't love her more if she were. To be that far away from her—I don't think I could stand it. Steven sent me a picture today. You should see how much she's grown just in the past few weeks!" She found the picture on her phone and handed it to him.

"She's pulling herself up already?" he said.

"Yes," Lily said. She took the phone back and smiled lovingly at the picture as she sat. Another tear crept out and she quickly wiped it away.

"So, New York it is, then," he said. "Assuming I ever get out of here."

She tucked a bit of wavy hair behind his ear. "Give yourself some time."

"I just hate feeling so..." He looked away.

Helpless, she thought. That's what he meant to say. He'd always been so healthy and strong, so independent. He rarely ever had a cold or the flu. To suddenly be taken down, betrayed by his own body, it had to be killing him.

"Hey," she said sympathetically, easing onto the bed next to him.

149

He turned back and gave her a rueful smile. He raised his left arm for her to snuggle closer to him, but was quiet.

"I know what it's like, you know? I felt the same way after the accident. Powerless. Frustrated. But you'll get through it. I know you will."

What if I don't? He thought it, but he didn't allow himself to speak the words. He held her for a while, before forcing himself to speak again. "Lily..."

"Hmm?" she said wearily.

"You should probably get going before we both fall asleep."

"No."

"Hmm?"

"I'm not leaving," she said calmly.

"Lily..."

"Tony, I can't. I need to be with you."

"Okay," he conceded with a weak smile. As much as he might have wanted to be alone, to wallow in self-pity, he was just as glad she refused to leave. He needed her to stay tonight, needed her optimism, needed to feel her next to him, to feel like everything was going to be okay, if only for a little while.

"I can move if you're not comfortable."

"No," he said, holding her more tightly.

She took hold of his free hand, weaving her fingers around the pulse monitor on his finger.

"Bonne nuit, mon amour. Je t'aime," he said softly as he kissed her forehead.

"Je t'aime aussi," she said, drifting off.

So much for tomorrow being better.

"Bugger!" Tony said. He flung his copy of *Men's Fitness* across the room just as Lily came in.

She eyed him in the chair as she bent to retrieve it.

"Sorry," he said.

"You all right?" she asked.

He shrugged, looking down.

She scanned the cover while quietly sipping her tea and noted the article on training for a triathlon. She glanced up at him. "Do you want to talk about it?"

"Not really," he said. He pushed himself out of the chair.

Seeing him start to falter, Lily dropped the magazine onto the bedside table and reached out to help him.

He sighed and took her hands, disgusted with himself.

"Thank you," he murmured as she helped him onto the edge of the bed.

He'd been doing his best to play tough, but Lily recognized the pain in his eyes. "It's gonna be okay, you know?" she said, stepping between his legs. "You heard what the doctor said this morning."

"I know," he nodded. "I think I just need some time to get used to... everything."

"Yes, you do," she said. She caressed his stubbly cheek.

"I also need a shave," he said, trying to sound more cheerful. "Maybe tomorrow." He took her hand and raised it to his lips.

They gazed at each other, quiet for a few moments until Lily stepped away and shook her head.

"What's the matter?"

"Nothing. Just a bit of a headache." Her fingers worked at the base of her skull. "I thought I'd got rid of it, but I guess not."

"Have you eaten?" he asked, his forehead creased with concern. "Maybe you should take a break. Get some lunch."

"I don't need a break. I'm fine.

"I just don't want you wearing down and getting sick because of me."

"I'm fine," she assured him, wrapping her arms around his neck.

His hands came to rest on her hips and found that her jeans hung looser than usual, which did nothing to lessen his concern.

"Am I interrupting anything?" came a voice from the doorway.

"Danny!" Lily shouted, running toward him. She threw her arms around him. "What are you doing here? I thought you were busy."

"Well, you said you wished I were here. So, I cleared my schedule for a few days."

"It's good to see you," Tony said, putting out his hand and smiling the first genuine smile Lily had seen in days.

Danny approached him and took his hand, then leaned in to hug him.

"I'm sorry I couldn't get here sooner."

"No worries, mate," Tony said as he patted Danny on the back.

"How are you?"

"I've been better."

"Is there anything I can do?" Danny asked.

"If you can get your sister to eat something, you'd be doing me a huge favor."

"Done."

"Ugh! I'm not even hungry," Lily said.

"Fine. You can watch me eat. Let's go," Danny said, grabbing her jacket off the back of the chair.

Lily glanced back at Tony.

"Go on, then," Tony encouraged. "My favorite rehab therapist will be in any moment to see that I get my workout," he said. "If you can call it that."

"Piper?" Lily asked.

"That's the one."

"She's pretty," she teased him.

"She's angry!" he laughed. "Go!" he added with a wave of his hand.

"Yes, please! I'm starved," Danny said, tugging on her hand. "Tony, can we bring you anything?"

Tony shook his head and waved them off.

"I love you," Lily said, heading for the door.

"I love you too, angel," he called as they disappeared from view. He let out a loud sigh and settled back onto the bed.

A moment later, his phone rang. He picked it up, expecting to see his mother's number, but was pleasantly surprised by the name on the display.

"Hello, Gracie," he said. "It's nice to hear from you."

* * *

Lily suggested the Mexican grill around the corner from the medical center. Danny agreed to try it with only a minor amount of complaining.

"Forgive me. I'm just not a huge fan of tacos," he moaned as they took their seats at the high top table in the corner.

"Ha! Well, good job you ordered the chorizo. I'm sure you'll find it more to your liking," she teased.

"Very funny! My sister the wise ass!" he said, nearly choking.

"Sorry!" she laughed. "Oh, Danny... I've missed you so much!" she said. She reached across the table to touch him lovingly on the arm.

"I've missed you too," he said, patting her hand.

"How long can you stay?" she asked.

"That depends. How long do you suppose Steven can handle things without me?"

"How is Steven? How's Josie?"

"They're both fine. Wonderful, actually. She misses you."

"I miss her, too. So much," Lily said as she took another bite from her fajita bowl.

Danny knew her well enough to know that she would continue with small talk and pleasantries as long as possible, so he jumped at the chance to change the subject while she chewed.

"Never mind us. How is Tony doing, really?"

She swallowed and wiped her hands extensively on her paper napkin to delay the conversation, if only for a few more seconds. She knew she wouldn't be able to hide her emotions from him. When her napkin was all but worn through, she licked her lips and cleared her throat. "The last couple of days have been tough on him. But, we had a visit from the doctor this morning, so at least we know more of our options."

"Which are?"

"Well, they still can't be sure of exactly why the kidney stopped working. They've seen to it that he's well hydrated. They've run tests to rule out infection and things. It could just be reacting to the trauma of surgery. But right now we're just waiting to see if it will start up again on its own. And until it does..."

"Dialysis."

She nodded.

"And what if it doesn't? Is there a chance of a transplant or something?"

She shook her head. "Not really. We could try it, but chances are that the drugs they're going to use to fight the cancer—the immunotherapy in particular—would increase the risk of rejection. If it comes down to it, he may be able to do something called Automated Peritoneal Dialysis."

"What's that?"

"They put a catheter into the abdomen which you attach to a machine every night before you go to bed. Then the machine exchanges the fluids while you sleep. It takes about eight to ten hours, but supposedly one can lead a relatively normal life that way."

"Sounds like a pretty good alternative."

"Yeah," she said with a shrug.

"You're not convinced?"

"No. I am. It's just... He's still having a hard time adjusting to the idea. I know how he feels, though." She poked at her food. "Sometimes it doesn't matter how good the alternatives are or how bad it could have been. Sometimes you know you should be thankful, and you are, but there's this moment after a diagnosis..." She paused, lost in thought or memory, then continued "...a moment when you realize you'll never be quite the same person ever again. And you can't help but mourn the loss of that person. You can't help but wonder if you'll look the same, or walk the same. If you'll dance the same or make love the same..."

"Speaking of—" he changed the subject again "Have a look at those two!" He motioned toward a couple making out in the corner.

"Good Lord!" she said, putting another fork full of chicken and peppers into her mouth.

"I miss being kissed like that," Danny said.

"So do I!" Lily said, hiding her mouth with her hand as she chewed.

"How long's it been?" he asked.

"Danny!"

"Come on!"

"Three weeks."

"Oh! You poor thing!" Danny said dramatically. "Well, you won't be only one. I left mine in New York for the week. Not that it matters much."

"Oh? Is everything okay with you and Steven?"

"Yes. Fine. There's just no time now that we have Jocelyn. And even when there is time, we're both so tired that we'd rather go to sleep, you know? It just doesn't seem worth the energy. And the one night we did manage to get it together, we forgot to lock the door and..."

Danny launched into a story, but Lily was suddenly more interested in something across the room.

"Here, what are you looking at now?" he asked when he realized she wasn't responding. "Lily?"

"What? Oh, sorry. I just... I thought I recognized someone."

"Who?"

"There was a woman. I thought I saw her in the carpark at the hospital, too."

"Where is she?"

"She's gone now. Never mind. What were you saying?"

"Mrs. Lebowitz!" he said.

"What about her?"

"She walked in on us while we were on the job!"

"How?"

"She was looking for her damn cat! When we didn't answer..."

"Who does that?"

"I know!"

"Well, it could have been worse."

"What could be worse than being caught starkers by Ida Lebowitz?"

"It could have been Steven's mother."

"Bloody hell!"

"Right? Like the time Maggie heard Tony and me shaggin' in 'is room?"

"What?"

"Yes! When we went over for a visit just before we moved out here."

"You never told me about that!"

"That was the night the casting agent called about the *Last Dance* contract, which Tony announced at breakfast the next morning. Do you know what she said? In that high, calm voice of hers... 'Judging by the level of excitement we heard coming from your room last night, I'm guessing she got the part!' I almost died of embarrassment."

Danny snorted with laughter.

"She also accused me of being a good actress, if you know what I mean!"

"Is that what it is? Acting? I mean, does he just like to hear you?" Danny asked as he took another bite.

"Tony? No. And with him it's no act. Now, with Charles..." She tipped her head. "And he never knew the difference."

"The poor sod," Danny said. Then he noticed Lily fanning herself her hand. "What's the matter?"

"Is it warm in here or is it just me?"

"Just you. Or the jalapeños. One or the other."

"I think it's the salsa. It's quite spicy, isn't it?"

"Not really," he laughed.

She laughed too, but before long her laughter subsided and her face began to pucker as she tried to suppress the tears.

"That salsa's making your eyes water," Danny said, making light. He handed her another napkin.

She dropped her fork into her half empty bowl and pushed it away. "Sorry," she said as she dabbed at the water in the corners of her eyes. "God! Lately I just feel like it's a constant struggle to hold my shit together." She ran her fingers through her hair. "Do you have any idea what I would give to have him home with me again, to hold him in my arms to..."

"Lil," Danny said soothingly.

"I just can't bear the thought of losing him," she said, swallowing the last word.

"He's going be okay, Sissy. You have to believe that." He reached across the table for her.

"I'm trying. Really, I am."

"Hey, you gave us a scare a time or two and look at you, hmm?" He squeezed her hand.

"Right." She gave him a tentative smile then glanced at his watch. "I guess we should get back, shouldn't we?" she said as she slid off her stool. "We're not that far away. Would you mind walking?"

"Not at all." He stood and held out his arm and she linked hers through it.

"Danny, thank you so much for coming here to be with me. You have no idea... how much it means," she said as they started down the sidewalk.

"You and me, Sis. Always. You know that."

She smiled. "Forever," she said, leaning her head on his for just a second.

"Lil?"

"Hmm?"

"Is there something else you're not telling me?"

"I'm just glad you're here. That's all. It's nice to have someone on my side."

"On your side?"

"Yeah. You know. Tony's family has been here, but..."

"Ah ha! Trouble with the in-laws?"

"That's just it. They're not really my in-laws, are they? And after everything that's happened..."

"Maggie still hasn't warmed to you since your reunion?"

"No. And we used to be so close. I guess I hoped we might find our way back to the way things were, despite everything. I mean, I expected it to take time, but lately... things seem even worse."

"Well, don't read too much into it. She's worried about her son."

"I suppose so."

"I know so. If it were Jocelyn—"

"Shh! Don't even put that out there."

"Well, you can imagine."

"Mmm," Lily nodded. Only she couldn't imagine. No matter how much she wished she could.

They walked for a while without speaking until Lily stopped and turned around to look behind her.

"What is it?" Danny asked.

Lily looked puzzled. "Nothing, I guess."

"Less than a month back in Hollywood and you're convinced the paparazzi are following you," Danny joked.

Lily gave him an uneasy smile. "Hardly. Hollywood is more interested in Charles than in me," she said, moving forward again.

"Well, someone must be interested. You've had quite a few job opportunities lately," Danny said.

"True."

"Speaking of which... I ran into Justine Sorenson a couple of days ago. She asked me to tell you hello."

"That's nice. How's her show coming along?"

"She said it's going well."

"Good."

"She also said she wished you were in it."

"What? I would have loved to do it. She was the one who told me it wasn't going to work."

"From what she said, I got the impression that she thought you were already on contract with someone else."

Lily frowned at him, obviously questioning the idea.

"I don't know," Danny shrugged in answer. "Maybe you should call her."

"I don't suppose it matters much at this point, does it? Come on," she said, her step quickening as if just realized she'd been away far too long.

17
REALITY CHECK

Several days later Lily sat in the lounge waiting for Tony to complete his third round of dialysis.   Their earlier conversation replayed in her head.

"I still haven't heard anything from Justine. I just don't get it. Why would she think that I already had a job?"

"Maybe someone told her that you did."

"Agnes wouldn't have told her that. Who would have told her that?"

"I have one idea."

"Who?"

He'd given her a look then. *"Who else?"* he'd said. *"Charles!"*

She couldn't believe Tony would even suggest such a thing. Charles was no saint. That was for certain, but he'd been more than helpful lately with regard to her career. To accuse him of that kind of sabotage was unfair. She didn't even want to acknowledge the idea, yet she was tempted to text Charles to ask him if he'd had anything to do with it, if for no other reason than to disprove Tony's theory.

She sighed loudly as her fingers worked at the base of her skull, thankful to be alone in the quiet room. After a few minutes, she dragged herself out of the chair. She hoped that a cup of coffee might help to clear her head.

"Good morning, Lil."

She looked up. "Oh, Eric. Good morning."

"I just stopped in to discuss follow-up treatment with Tony. He told me you were down here."

"How is he doing?" she asked.

"He's doing as well as can be expected. Actually, he's more concerned about you."

She sighed again. "Well, he needn't be. I'm fine." She took a sip of coffee and swallowed it with some difficulty.

He smiled. "Come on," he said, putting an arm around her shoulder. "Take a walk with me. Let me buy you a decent cup of coffee."

* * *

They took a seat in an empty corner of the cafeteria with fresh coffee and frosted cinnamon rolls. Dr. Channing immediately started in on a roll, claiming that they were some of the best he'd ever had, despite their place of origin. He nudged the other roll toward her and she shook her head, looking ill at the thought.

"Are you sure? They're delicious."

"No, thank you. The thought of all of that icing is..." she turned up her nose.

"I can get you something else. A fruit plate or—"

"Eric, I don't need anything. I had a yogurt earlier."

"Ok," he said in surrender.

"So, tell me," she started. "How are you and Cecily doing?"

"Good. We're leaving for Cabo later today."

"Just the two of you?"

"Mmm hmm. Just a few days, but..."

"That's great. It sounds like the two of you have found a way to work through your differences?"

He raised an eyebrow and gave a half-smile. "We're trying, anyway."

"It's not always easy, is it?"

He shook his head. "No, it's not. It's taken a lot of work to get this far. And I've had to come to some pretty big realizations."

"Such as?"

"Well, you know, she's an entertainment reporter. Gossip is her business. It's not mine, and I don't always like her methods, but I can't ask her to be less than she is."

"As long as she keeps it legal."

"Exactly!"

"I can't say that I always agreed with everything Charles did either," she laughed. "But he is brilliant."

"He is. But he wasn't good enough for you."

"What?"

"Now that you're divorced I can say that to you. I never thought he was good enough for you. Tony seems like a much better fit."

She nodded. "He is."

"He's worried about you, Lil."

"Well, I'm worried about him, so…"

"Tell me about your headaches."

She rolled her eyes. "You too, now?"

"Lily, talk to me."

"Eric, it's just a headache."

"Severe?"

"Not really."

"Scale of one to ten."

She sighed, aggravated. "You're not gonna give up on this, are you?"

"No."

"I don't know. Three. Maybe four. They're not that bad."

"Intermittent or constant?"

"Not constant."

"But recurring?"

"Yes."

"How long?"

"Just a few days now. I'm sure it's nothing. Probably just stress."

"Maybe. Maybe not. Have you experienced unusual fatigue?"

She tilted her head. "Yes."

"What about loss of appetite? I'm guessing yes."

"Yes," she said almost inaudibly.

"Weight loss?"

"That is normal when you're not eating! Eric, come on! Everything you've just described... they're all perfectly normal for someone under a great deal of stress. I'm not sleeping well. I'm not eating. The man I love has been in and out of hospital and I'm absolutely sick about it. It doesn't have to mean..." She couldn't say it out loud. "I would know, wouldn't I? I mean, I would... know. If it were..."

"Maybe I'm over-reacting," he admitted. "But given your history, I'd sure as hell rather find out I'm wrong than let this go unchecked and find out it's another tumor."

"Christ, Eric!" she said shaking her head.

As usual, he cut right to the chase.

She pressed her lips together. "It's nothing," she said quietly.

He reached across the table and took her hand. "I hope you're right, Lil. But I care about you too much to let you take chances with your health."

She avoided eye contact as she took a moment to let his words sink in. Then, she slowly fished a tissue from her purse and dabbed her eyes. After she blew her nose she looked up at him. "Okay, Doctor. What now?"

18
WHAT NEXT?

Lily finished her business with Eric and returned to Tony's room just as he was signing his discharge papers. He couldn't have been more pleased to be escaping the confines of his medically induced incarceration, even if he did have to promise to return for out-patient dialysis.

For the remainder of the morning Lily threw herself into caring for him to take her mind off of everything else.

By the afternoon, though, her vigilance became a bit too much for Tony.

"You know, you don't actually have to sit and wait for me," he said as he came out of the master bath.

"I just thought I'd sit here and read. In case you needed anything."

"Lily, I was taking a shower, not running a marathon. I can manage." He hung his towel on the rack and set about shaving, carefully avoiding the catheter and the area of his neck still covered by the plastic shower shield.

She watched him from her chair. He was wearing his favorite pair of navy jogging pants. They were her favorite, too. She loved the way they hung on his hips. The weeks without exercise had taken some toll, but he still looked quite good. She noticed that his incisions were really healing nicely—more quickly than hers had, if she remembered correctly. Then again, she'd had so many surgeries after the accident that it was hard to recall the specifics. And the last one to remove the tumor on her spine...

"Damn!" he hissed.

"Are you all right? You didn't nick the line, did you?"

"Everything is fine, darling. Just a small cut. No need to call the ambulance."

"Was that supposed to be funny?"

"No. Just trying to put your concerns at bay."

"Darling, can I help it if I'm worried about you after what you've been through?"

"No. But you've been watching me like a hawk, Lil. You know it makes me crazy."

"Fine. I'm sorry." She stood up. "I'll be on the balcony if you need me," she said, sneaking in to give him a quick kiss on the cheek. "You missed a spot."

"Where?" he turned to look and knocked the razor on the floor. He made a move to pick it up.

She put a hand on his chest. "No bending yet," she reminded him.

He sighed heavily.

169

"Would you just... let me help you?" She picked up the razor, gently turned his cheek toward the light with his chin in her hand, and cleaned up the last bit of stubble. "There," she said, smiling sweetly. She gazed at him for a moment, then whispered, "I love you." She kissed him softly and turned to leave.

He thought he saw a tear in her eye. "Lily?" he said.

"Let me know if you need anything else," she said, and out she went.

As she sat on the balcony staring out over Hollywood Hills, she could hear Tony faintly through the glass doors. He was obviously on a business call. He would periodically appear in the sitting room and then disappear again, pacing slowly as he talked. When she could no longer hear his conversation, she went in to check on him.

"Hey," he said from his spot on the bed.

"Did you wear yourself out with all of that pacing?"

"I guess I did," he chuckled. "Thanks," he said as she handed him a fresh bottle of water. He opened it and took a long drink.

"I assume that was Sam on phone?"

He nodded. "And Mum called, of course."

"Mmm. Any progress with the performing arts center?" she asked, taking a seat next to him.

"I sent the updated plans to Sam and he met with the foundation. They've accepted them and are ready to begin construction."

"That's great!"

"Yes, it is. At this point, I'm just hoping I'll be able to make it over there for the opening ceremony."

"Of course you will. That's months away."

"I don't know."

"Hey, it's not every day you land a *royal* project. We are going to do everything in our power to make sure you're there when the princess cuts that ribbon."

He smiled then and reached out for her hand. "Thank you."

"You don't have to thank me," she said.

"All right. Then I'm thankful *for* you. I don't know what I would do without you."

She gazed at him and smiled faintly before averting her eyes.

"Lil, are you all right?" he asked.

She could hear Eric's words again now. *Tell him.* She wanted to tell him. To lean on him. She needed his strength. But he needed hers more. He'd been through so much already. It didn't make sense to worry him—at least not until she knew something for sure.

She studied the thread pattern on the duvet for several seconds before looking back up at him. "Tony," she said in her calmest, steadiest voice, "I don't want you to worry about me. The best thing you can do for me... is to concentrate on getting better. Stronger. So you can take the next steps, whatever those might be. Okay?"

He stared at her for a moment. Then he pulled the hand he was holding to his chest, forcing her to lean toward him. "Okay," he whispered. He kissed her softly, first on the forehead then on each cheek before reaching her mouth.

It was a kiss so lovely and tender that the world would have melted away, had it not been for the nagging pain at the back of her head and the ball of anxiety in her stomach.

"Someday I'd like to take the next step with you," he said.

"What's that?"

"Well, when all of this is over," he said and gave a dramatic pause. Then he took a deep breath and looked into her eyes. "I want to marry you."

She felt her chest tighten. She'd waited years to hear those words from him. But now? She was in no position to make any promises.

She laughed nervously. Then, for lack of a better way to respond, she leaned over and kissed him again. She kissed him long enough and hard enough that she hoped it might distract him and sat back to smile at him.

He grinned and eased onto his side, allowing room for her to lie next to him.

As their bodies pressed together gently, she could feel other areas of his body preparing to demand more attention than his brain.

"God, Lily," he said as he kissed her neck. "I want so badly to make love to you right now, but there isn't a damn thing I can do about it."

"I think there might be something I can do about it," she said as her fingertips slipped under the waistband of his pants.

With Tony satisfied and resting, Lily excused herself and went out to the sitting room. She approached the butler's pantry with the idea of making a cup of tea, but as she was about to pick up the electric kettle, she noticed her phone sitting there. Out of habit, she picked it up and hit the display button to check for any notifications.

There was a missed call and a voicemail from Eric. Her heart jumped into her throat at the sight of his name. She took a breath and swallowed before listening to his message.

"Lil, call me as soon as you get this. We need to talk about your bloodwork."

She felt sick. She rushed into the powder room and closed the door. She gripped the edge of the washbowl, forcing herself to breath until the initial panic subsided. When she was able to move again, she closed the lid and sat on the toilet. She pressed the call back button and dialed Eric.

Several minutes later Lily came back into the bedroom.

Tony looked up from his book.

She had her coat on and was fumbling around in her purse.

"What's up?" he asked.

"I have to go out for a little while," she said from behind her designer sunglasses.

173

"Is everything all right?"

"Fine. Just something I need to deal with. Will you be okay?"

"Sure. But..."

"If you need anything, you'll call your mum?"

"Okay."

She looked back at him from the doorway and blew him a kiss. "I love you."

"I love you too," he called after her.

In the hallway she rang Danny for the second time. Still no answer.

Feeling desperate, she dialed the phone again.

After three rings, he picked up. "Oh, thank God," she said. "I need to talk to you."

19
UNDENIABLE EVIDENCE

Lily awoke the next morning to the sound of
someone pounding on the hotel room door.
She roused herself as quickly as she could,
grabbed a robe to cover her shorty nightgown
and rushed toward the door, one hand holding
the back of her head.

"Danny, what the hell?" she said when she
saw him standing there.

"Have you seen your Twitter feed?" he
asked as he pushed past her.

"Good morning to you too," she said.

"Sorry. No time for pleasantries. We have a
problem!"

"What?"

"More specifically, you have a problem. Or
Tony's going to."

"What? Tony's fine." she said, confused.

"He might not be when he hears about
this."

"What are you talking about?"

"You were with Charles last night."

She sighed. "Danny..."

"At his house."

"I..."

"You hugged him. You kissed him, for Christ sake, Lil!"

"Yes but... No! He kissed *me* goodnight! But it wasn't that kind of kiss. How the hell do you know that?"

"Everyone knows about it, darling. It's all over TMZ, for God's sake!" He flashed her the picture that was on his phone. "What the hell were you thinking?"

She grabbed it out of his hand and eyed the photo. "Bloody hell!" she said as she scrolled through his feed. "Are they in the papers too?"

"Not front page," he said, proffering the copy of *L.A. Times* opened to the incriminating evidence.

She grabbed it. "How the hell do they manage to make a kiss like that look like... like this!" she said, waving the paper around.

"Clever camera angles and editing?" Danny said.

"I think I'm gonna be sick," Lily said. She leaned against the back of the sofa, once again holding her head with one hand. The other still clutched the newspaper as she wrapped her arm around her middle.

"Good God, are you hung over?"

"No! I had one drink."

"What's going on with you?"

"Nothing. I'm fine. Just give me a minute."

"Lil, you're not actually involved with him again, are you?"

Lily closed her eyes and breathed out slowly. "Daniel Christopher, I'm not even going to dignify that with an answer."

"I had to ask. Here," he said, handing her a bottle of water from the mini fridge.

She took several gulps from the bottle before speaking again. "Danny, it isn't what it looks like."

"Then, what the hell is it?"

"I went there because—" She fell silent as Tony appeared from the bedroom.

"Good morning," he said.

Lily licked her lips.

Danny cleared his throat.

"What's going on?" Tony asked.

There was no point in trying to hide it. She slowly, reluctantly extended her hand offering him the *Times*. She watched the muscles in his jaw clench at the sight of the image before him.

He walked slowly to the sofa and lowered himself onto it.

She was frozen in place as he read the article, praying his reaction would be reasonable.

When he was finished, he turned to look at her, his eyes harsh and unyielding. He stood and dropped the paper on the coffee table.

"It's not what it looks like. I swear!" she cried as he crossed the room.

As he stood in front of the wall of glass staring out she approached him, taking hold of him, her hands resting on his biceps.

"Tony..." Her lips brushed over the muscles in his left shoulder. "Say something."

He rotated his shoulder, shaking her off. "What do you want me to say, Lily?" He shook his head. "I mean... really? What the fuck do you want me to say?"

Danny took a few steps back in an attempt to blend in with the potted silk plant in the corner, wishing he could somehow escape without being noticed.

Tony continued. "Just how many times do you expect me to fall for that same scenario? Hmm? You caught kissing him? How many times do you want me to believe that there is nothing going on between the two of you? God dammit, Lily! I can't do this anymore!"

Lily saw the color rising in Tony's face, the tension in his jaw. "Don't say that. Please. It wasn't that kind of kiss," she assured him.

"Lily..." He came toward her, mouth open, as if he were going to say something else. But, half way across the room he stopped and side-stepped, taking hold of the back of a chair.

Lily watched his face suddenly go white. "Tony?"

"I can't... I can't..." His free hand clutched at his chest.

She rushed toward him.

"Are you all right? Here. Sit down," she said.

He did.

"What's wrong?"

He shook his head.

"Tony, talk to me." She knelt in front of him. "What's happening?"

"Don't... know." He struggled to get the words out. "Can't... breathe."

"Are you in pain?"

He nodded slightly as he gasped for air. "My... chest..."

Lily stood and started to go for her phone.

"Lily..." Tony managed, reaching out for her.

She knelt down again. "Okay. I'm here," she said. "Danny," she called. "Dial nine-one-one. Then go down and get Maggie and Joe."

"On it." Danny said, dialing.

"Tell them to get dressed," she added. Then she turned back to Tony. The terrified look on his face tortured her, but she forced herself to hold together. "Look at me." She took his face in her hands. "It's gonna be okay. You're gonna be okay. Hear me?"

He nodded.

Her own heart felt as if it were going to explode out of her chest, but she ignored it. Her forehead resting on his, she breathed with him, whispering calming words until the paramedics arrived.

20
AFTERMATH

Lily rode in the back of the ambulance, praying as Tony's hand clung to hers. Suddenly, the morning's news seemed small and unimportant. But all over world, others were waking up to images of her and her ex. Many of them would make way too much out of it. Agents. Fans. Critics. Maggie. And Cora.

* * *

Across town, she sat glaring at the pages of the entertainment section. The sight of Lily and Charles in a more-than-friendly embrace, the thought of his lips on hers... She could feel her blood pressure rising as anger bubbled within her.

For years she'd loved him from afar. For years she'd dreamed of sharing a life with him. At one point she'd actually believed it might be possible. But, somehow, there was Lily, ever-present and always in the way. Even in these pictures, even after the divorce, he still looked at Lily in a way that he'd never looked at her.

"Bitch!" she grumbled, still glowering. With a groan she tore off the piece of newsprint and slowly, methodically, turned it into a pile of confetti. She smiled then, feeling some degree of satisfaction.

Lily and Charles would have to be dealt with, she thought. If he couldn't see what a mistake he was making, then she would have to show him. There was no sense in wasting any more time. It was time to make her move.

She swept the shredded paper into the waste basket and took out the pen and notepad that were in the desk drawer. She jotted a quick note, pulled the sheet off the pad, and tucked the note in the envelope with the other items, sealing the envelope before rising.

Purse in hand, she gathered the pile of items on the desk and set about her list of tasks.

21
NO EXCUSES

"Where is he?" Maggie called as she burst into the waiting area.

Joe and Danny followed close behind.

Lily stopped pacing and pivoted to face them, her eyes red and puffy.

"We asked about him in Emergency and they said he was sent up here. What's going on?" Joe said.

"They're running some tests to find out for sure. Something to do with his heart."

"My God!" Maggie gasped.

"Was it a heart attack?" Danny asked.

Lily shook her head. "They don't think so."

"Thank heaven for that," Joe said.

"How did this happen?" Maggie said.

Lily looked to Danny as if he might come to her rescue, but he only stared back with a rather pained look on his face.

"Lily?" Joe said. His voice, though still kind, was beginning to register impatience.

Lily crossed the room and sat, placing her hands on her thighs to settle herself before speaking. She forced herself to make eye contact with Tony's parents, who were still staring at her expectantly.

Danny sat next to her and put a hand on hers.

She took a breath. "We were... talking. He got upset. One minute he was fine and the next... he couldn't breathe."

"That's it?" Maggie said.

"Yes. That's it. I don't know what it was or how—"

"You said he got upset. About what?" Maggie said.

Lily leaned forward and picked up the newspaper that had been conveniently abandoned on the table in front of her. Without a word, she opened it to the entertainment news and handed it to Maggie. "You'll hear it soon enough, I expect."

Joe read the title over his wife's shoulder.

Is Their Hollywood Love Story Really Over?

"Is it?" he asked. "Over?"

"Of course it is!" Lily said, aggravated.

Maggie, finished skimming the article, refolded the paper and tossed it onto the table as she walked away from them.

"Maggie," Lily said, standing to follow her. "I know it looks bad. But it's not what it looks like."

"Oh, please!" Maggie griped.

"It's Hollywood, for God's sake! Things are not always as they appear. I can explain it all if—"

183

Maggie whipped around to look at her then, arms folded, clearly awaiting further explanation.

Startled by the sudden movement, Lily took a breath and pressed her lips together before finishing her sentence. "...if you'll just give me the chance to explain it to Tony first."

At that, Maggie rolled her moistened eyes and refocused them on the floor.

"Maggie, please. I owe him that," Lily said. She couldn't be certain whether Maggie's expression was one of disgust or merely her attempt to fight a breakdown—something Lily herself had been doing for weeks.

"Look," Lily continued, "you can be angry at me. I don't blame you. You can blame me for everything that's happened. I don't care. It doesn't matter anymore what you think of me. The only thing that matters is Tony. I love him more than I've ever loved anyone, and the *only* thing I care about... is whether or not he's all right."

The two women stood as if locked in some kind of standoff, their eyes now doing all of the talking.

Joe and Danny had been watching the whole scene from across the room. They exchanged glances, each wondering if or when they should step in. Before they had a chance to make a move, a white coat appeared in the doorway.

"Excuse me," he said. "Ms. Josephson?"

"Yes," Lily said rushing toward him.

"I'm Dr. Skala, chief of cardiology." He motioned toward the row of faux leather chairs. "Shall we?"

"These are Tony's parents," Lily said as they moved to take their seats.

"What can you tell us, Doctor?" Joe asked after everyone had exchanged pleasantries.

Dr. Skala pulled one of the chairs around and sat facing the four of them. "Tony had an episode of arrhythmia."

"A what?" Maggie said.

"An irregular heart rhythm. In his case, it was bradycardia, a slow heart rate causing the angina and other symptoms. We've given him a dose of atropine. His heart seems to have regained a normal rhythm."

"So it definitely wasn't a heart attack?" Joe said.

"No. It only mimicked one," the doctor assured him.

Lily frowned. Tony was one of the most active men she knew, incredibly fit. He'd never had any issues with his heart. "What caused it?" she asked.

"Most likely, it was an effect of Cardiorenal Syndrome. A patient experiencing acute renal failure suddenly shows symptoms of acute heart failure or vice versa."

"Is it likely to happen again?" Maggie said.

"It's possible. We're keeping an eye on it. We're also watching his blood pressure. It's more elevated than we would like."

"What's the worst-case scenario?" Joe said.

"Worst case—if it's not kept under control— it could result in an actual heart attack or stroke."

Maggie leaned her head on her Joe's shoulder.

"We're doing everything we can to see that doesn't happen. Along those lines, Dr. Jones will be in later to discuss the next steps regarding the continuous dialysis."

Lily nodded. "Can we see him?" she asked.

"Of course. They're getting him set up in ICU now. Someone will let you know once he's settled."

* * *

Lily slipped into the room and stood while the nurse finished checking Tony's vitals. "Don't wear him out," she said with a smile as she passed Lily on her way out.

Lily nodded.

Once the nurse had gone, she approached Tony's bedside. "I'm so glad you're okay," she said.

"So am I," he said. "I'm glad you're here."

"Your mum and dad and Danny are here too," she said softly. "You had us all pretty worried." She reached out to touch his cheek.

He took hold of her hand and gently moved it away. Then he gazed into her eyes as if looking for an answer of some kind and finally said, "We need to talk."

Lily managed a weak smile.

"What do we do now?" he said.

186

She started in on what the doctor had said and about scheduling the surgery to put in the fistula for continuous dialysis.

He shook his head. "Lily, that's not what I mean and you know it. We need to talk about what happened. About us."

"We can talk later," she said. "You need to rest."

"No, Lily. Now."

His voice was soft. Melancholy. It sent an eerie shiver down her spine. Silly as it was, she'd rather hoped that the medical emergency would have overshadowed this morning's explosion. Clearly, he hadn't forgotten where they'd left off. She cleared her throat. "Okay," she said.

Tony looked at the woman standing before him. She was dressed in yoga pants and a pale blue lululemon hoodie with holes for the thumbs—clothes that she'd thrown on while the paramedics helped him onto the gurney. Her hair was thrown up, un-brushed, in a messy pony tail. Her face was plain. No make-up. No jewelry. She looked thin. Ashen. Tears were still welling in her eyes.

She sat on the edge of the chair next to his bed, her hands in her lap, looking at him anxiously. She reminded him now of the scared little girl he once knew and it broke his heart. He swallowed the lump in his throat.

"I don't know how to say this, really," he said. "I didn't think I ever would, but..."

"Tony..."

"Lil, I meant what I said earlier. I can't do this anymore. I can't go on like—"

"Tony, don't." Her bottom lip began to quiver. "I know you're upset. I don't blame you, but we can sort this out. They're just a bunch of stupid pictures," she said getting to her feet.

"It's not just about the pictures, Lil."

"I can explain everything. Just let me—"

"I'm sure you can," he sighed. "But let's face it. It would only be a matter of time before we were having this conversation all over again."

"Tony, I love you!"

"I know that!" he said, his voice rising. "I love you too. I expect I always will." He smiled slightly, but the worry lines around his eyes still showed. "But it's not enough."

"Of course it is."

"No." He shook his head. "It isn't. I wish it were. But, for whatever reason, you can't seem to imagine your life without him. And I can't seem to imagine a future for us with him in it. And that's a big problem."

"It doesn't have to be."

"It is... a problem," he repeated. "Unless..." He made eye contact to be sure he had her attention. "Unless you're prepared to cut all ties with him."

"Is that an ultimatum? Really, Tony. You know I can't do that."

"Can't? Or won't?"

"I can't and I won't. For one thing, that would be extremely detrimental to my career. And for another, he's done nothing wrong."

"Not that you would admit it if he had."

"What's that supposed to mean?"

"Do you have any idea how often you make excuses for him? No. You don't. Because it just comes naturally to you. Maybe it's just your personality. Or... maybe... you do it because deep down you really do still have feelings for him."

At that, her jaw clenched so tightly he thought she might break a tooth.

She took several controlled breaths before responding. "I care about him. I have never lied to you about that. But I didn't go there to *be* with him. I just needed to talk to him. As a friend."

"Rather than talk to the man who'd just proposed to you?" he said bitterly.

"No! It wasn't like that," she said, obviously frustrated. "If you'll just let me explain—"

"Lily, stop it! Please, just... stop. I don't want any more excuses. It doesn't matter why you went over there. It only matters that you did. The world still sees you as his potential love interest and that's exactly the way he wants it."

"Don't be ridiculous."

"I don't think I am. It doesn't even matter what *you* want. He obviously still wants you and I'd be willing to bet that he will do just about anything to get you back."

"He does not! We're friends, but that's all."

Tony pushed on. "For all we know, he might have set the whole damn thing up himself. I wouldn't put a damn thing past him."

"Oh!" she grumbled. "You make 'im sound like some kind of a monster."

"And you'll never see him for what he is."

"Good Lord! When the hell did you become so bloody insecure?"

His eyes darted around the room as he considered his surroundings and she instantly regretted those words.

"I'm sorry," she said, looking down.

He inhaled as the blood pressure cuff squeezed his arm again then seemed to sound an alarm. When it was finished, he continued. "Once I'm able to travel again, I'm going to go home."

"Of course you are. We'll both go."

"No, I mean I'm going to London... permanently."

Her mouth fell open.

"You can stay here or in New York, whichever you like. You're welcome to stay at the apartment—at least until you can make other arrangements."

She gulped down a sob and quickly wiped the stream of tears from her cheek with the back of her sleeve. "So that's it? Just like that?"

"Why make this any harder than it has to be?" he said.

"Why not? Why should I make it easy for you? Why should I let you throw away everything that we've fought for? Hmm? Why? Tell me!" she shouted from the foot of the bed.

The monitors began to beep faster. Moments later, another nurse, surlier than the last, charged into the room. "What's going on in here?"

"We're 'aving a discussion," Lily snapped.

"Well, you're going to have to wrap it up," the nurse said. "We can't have you agitating the patient."

"Could you just give us one second?" Lily said without making eye contact.

The nurse looked from one to the other.

"I don't think there's anything left to say," Tony said.

Lily took an audible breath. "Fine," she said as the other woman stood holding the door. "Just one thing before I go."

She approached, leaned over, and kissed him.

It took everything he had not to let himself be pulled into the kiss. His hands gripped the blanket at his sides to avoid reaching for her.

She pulled away, crushed. All of the tenderness they'd shared the night before seemed to have disappeared. She turned to leave, then paused another moment, willing him to say something else. Anything else. Something that might indicate there was still hope. But he didn't say a word.

"I love you," she said with one last look. "I'm not gonna let it end like this."

But there was no give in his face, his blue eyes like ice. "You don't have a choice," he said coldly.

Her stomach churned at the thought of walking away. But as much as she wanted to fight right now, she couldn't. She didn't know how. She didn't have the energy. She squeezed past the nurse in the doorway and stepped out.

He waited for the door to close behind them before allowing himself to let his guard down. He exhaled as his head hit the pillow. A wave of gut-wrenching sadness washed over him, and all he could do was close his eyes and pray that he'd just done the right thing. For both of them.

Outside Tony's room, Lily came face to face with Joe and Maggie, both looking guilty. She wondered just how much they'd overheard. Not wanting to give Maggie the satisfaction, she fought the emotions that threatened to tear her apart. "He's all yours," she said with a phony smile. "Where's Danny?"

"He went downstairs to call Steven," Joe said.

"Thank you," she whispered.

With nothing else to say, she made a move to walk away, but Joe stopped her.

"Lily, what just happened in there?" he asked.

"I don't know, really," Lily said with a blank stare.

She turned and slowly walked down the hallway, her hand skimming the wall, as if the wall were the only thing keeping her from falling over.

22
MAIL CALL

Charles looked up from his computer as Cora strolled in with his lunch and a stack of mail.

"Anything good?" he asked as she put his sandwich down in front of him.

She flipped through the stack. "Looks like some fan letters, a card from Robert Mitchell, the bill from the gardeners. The usual," she said. "This one feels like a photo."

"Is it the publicity shot from Jackie? Let me see?" he reached out his hand.

She gave him the large manila envelope and the card from Robert and walked over to her desk with the rest of the mail. "I take it you saw the news?" she said, eyeing the copy of the *Times* lying next to his laptop.

"I take it you did, too," he said.

"I did."

"And? What did you think?"

She sat in her desk chair and swiveled to face him. "What am I supposed to say to that?"

"Whatever you want to say." He waited.

She stared for a moment, then shrugged and said, "I don't know what to say." She turned back toward her desk and took out the check registry.

"Did you pick up my suit for tomorrow?" he asked as he took the letter opener out of his desk drawer and sliced open the photo envelope.

"Yes," she said with a laugh.

"What?" he said, surprised by her reaction.

"The woman at the dry cleaners actually asked me if I thought there was any hope of the two of you getting back together."

"Really? What did you tell her?"

"I told her I couldn't say. Then I left."

"Oh."

She spun back around. "Pretty ballsy, don't you think? Considering that most of the city thinks you and I are in some kind of a relationship."

He raised an eyebrow. The acidic nature of her comment did not escape him, but he chose to ignore it. "I guess," he said.

"But then, maybe that's the problem," she added.

"What is?"

"We're not really in a relationship, are we? We never were."

"Baby," he said, "you know that I—"

"Don't," she said. "Don't 'baby' me."

"Cora," he said with a sigh.

"And don't try to gloss over this like it's no big deal."

"What do you want from me?"

195

"I want you to be brave. That's what I want. I want you to man up and admit that you still love her. I want you to be honest with her—with everyone—for once. And this game we're playing... I don't want to do it anymore!"

She watched his eyes considering her, calculating his next move. She waited for him to speak, but he said nothing. Instead, he pulled the photo from the envelope and consulted the slip of paper that fell out.

"Shit," she heard him mumble.

She stood and nervously tucked her hair behind one ear. "I think maybe it would be better for me to move out," she said.

"Come on."

"I'm serious. My parents aren't getting any younger. Maybe it's time I went home."

"Fuck," he whispered, still staring at the picture. He tore his eyes off of it just in time to watch her walk head down out of the office.

"Fuck!" he said again. He sprang from behind his desk and dashed after her. "Cora!"

23
TIME WILL TELL

"Lily," the man shouted as he thrust the recorder in her face, "Can you give us your reaction to this morning's news?"

"Charles George and I are friends and colleagues. That's all," Lily said.

"Mr. George was unavailable for comment. What do you suppose he's thinking?"

She knew exactly what he was thinking. Unavailable for comment was his way of stirring the pot, of generating publicity. Good or bad, he had to keep them talking. He could always deny at a later date. But she couldn't tell them that. She faked a smile and said with a flutter of laughter, "I'm sure I don't know what Charles is thinking. He is no longer my concern. I have bigger things to worry about right now."

"Like what?" a woman called as she pushed her way toward the front of the crowd.

"*That*," Lily said emphatically, "is none of *your* concern. If you'll excuse me," she said as Danny pulled up in his rental car.

"How does your boyfriend feel about your so-called friendship with Mr. George?" someone called after her.

"No further comment, thank you," she said as she climbed into the passenger seat and closed the door. But the question echoed in her head, taunting her all the way back to the hotel.

When she and Danny arrived at the hotel, Lily excused herself, claiming she was in desperate need of a nap. They both knew that was only partially true. What she really wanted was a chance to cry her eyes out without an audience. Danny respectfully took his leave, but kept her key and promised to check on her in an hour. Sure enough, when, an hour later, she emerged from the shower freshly dressed and blown dry, he was there on the sofa with a bucket of beer and a large cheese pizza.

"Join me?" he asked, raising a bottle of Blue Moon.

"Why not," she said. She took a seat facing him with one foot folded beneath her. "Where did that come from?" she asked, eyeing the large fruit basket on table.

"I don't know. I found it outside your door. The card says 'I watch you all the time.'"

"There are nesting dolls in it!" she laughed.

"With ballerinas on them!" he added as she pulled the wooden dolls out of the cellophane.

"And this one's got a broken leg, poor thing." she said, holding tiniest one.

"It's cracked? That's a shame," Danny said.

"I swear... fans send the weirdest things, don't they? It's crazy!"

"But..." he said, opening a second bottle and handing it to her. "If it weren't for those crazies, we'd be out of a job!"

"Too true. To the crazies," she said as in a toast.

They touched the necks of the bottles together and each took a drink.

"Oh, God," Lily said, and her face puckered.

"Sorry. I know it's not your beverage of choice, but the thought of a whiskey with pizza..." He shook his head.

"It's fine," she said. "I just wasn't ready for it on an empty stomach." She stuck her tongue out in a retching gesture.

"I got you a salad," he said, motioning to the plastic container on the table.

"Thank you," she said. She set the beer aside. "Actually, do you mind if I steal a slice?"

"Not at all."

She reached for the pizza in hopes that putting something in her stomach would alleviate the nausea, if not the hollow, empty feeling.

"Drowning your sorrows in carbs?"

She smiled. "Something like that."

They had several bites without any comment until Danny's curiosity got the better of him.

"So?" he said, hesitating.

"Hmm?"

"What the fuck?"

"What the fuck," she repeated with a sigh.

"He really broke up with you?"

She chewed methodically without making eye contact, then swallowed and wiped her mouth. "It looks that way," she said.

"Is he serious?"

"He's angry and hurt. I'm sure he thinks this is what he wants."

She took another swallow of beer. It didn't sit any better with her than the last.

"What are you gonna do?" Danny said.

"The only thing I can do. Wait twenty-four hours and pray that he comes to his senses."

"Do you think he's right? About Charles?"

"Really?" she said in disbelief. Agitated and slightly sickened by the lingering smell of the beer, she got up and went into the powder room, where she emptied the bottle into the sink.

"It's not out of the question, is it?" Danny called from the other room. "Lil?" he said as she returned with the empty bottle.

"Yes, Daniel! It *is* out of the question." She slammed the bottle down on the counter of the butler's pantry. "Do you really think Charles would expose himself and his home—his private sanctuary—to the paparazzi?"

"Maybe."

"Then you don't know him like I do," she said as she sat back down with a bottle of water from the fridge.

"You might be right."

"But?" she snapped, certain there was one.

"But he did profess his love for you on national television."

"When was that?"

"His acceptance speech at the Oscars? Lizzie?"

Lily blushed. "How did you know?"

"Just a guess. But you just confirmed it. And if you think Tony didn't come to the same conclusion, you're underestimating him."

"Okay," she said after a minute. "You're right about that. Charles still cares about me. I still care about him. But he's been nothing but supportive through all of this. He's not the bad guy here, all right? It's not as if I was coerced into going over there. I went on my own accord. It was my idea. If this is anyone's fault, it's mine."

"Wow."

"What?"

"Nothing," he said. "Just that you used to make the same excuses for Dad."

"Daniel..." She gave him a look that said, "drop it."

"Fine. So, why did you go there?" he said.

"I just went to talk to him. That's all."

"Why him?"

She licked her lips. "I tried to reach you, but you were out and I... It couldn't wait. He was the only other one who knew." She blinked as her eyes began to tear and somehow he instantly knew.

"Shit," he said. "Tony was right to worry. You are sick. It's the cancer, isn't it?" he said, alarmed.

She nodded. "It might be. We ran some tests, but I won't know anything until Monday."

"Why so long? Can't they do a blood test or something? Isn't that faster?"

"Yes. They did. And I'm sure the results are in by now. But I asked Eric to handle it personally. Confidentiality, you know? And he's gone to Mexico for a romantic weekend. I haven't been able to get in touch with him."

"Shit, Sissy!"

She reached for his hand. "Listen, I don't want you to worry, okay? I mean, we don't know anything for sure, and even if it is... that doesn't mean—"

"Oh my God! Tony doesn't know, does he? That's what you wanted to explain."

She nodded again.

"How?"

She shook her head. "I never meant for it to be a secret. It just... never came up."

"Why not?"

"We were busy. Happy. It's not as if I live every day of my life waiting for a relapse." She paused and sighed. "When he got sick, I wanted to tell him—to let him know he wasn't alone. But he's always been so protective of me. He would only have worried and—"

"You have to tell him."

"Maybe subconsciously I wanted to be the strong one. For once. I don't know."

"Lil, you have to tell him," he repeated.

"I know that! God, Daniel, don't you think I know that?" She pushed herself off of the sofa.

Danny took a moment and then followed her out on to the balcony. He put an arm around her and rested his head on hers. "I'm sorry. I don't mean to judge."

"I know," she said, leaning her head on his shoulder. "I have made a real hash of it, haven't I?"

He said nothing, but his silence was affirmation enough.

"I don't know how in the world I can expect Tony to forgive me," she said.

"He loves you."

"I know he does. But even if he can get over this thing with Charles, I'm not sure he'll be able to get past the fact that I didn't tell him about my cancer. No matter what my reason was."

They stood there for quite some time letting the breeze and the sounds of distant traffic fill the silence. Occasionally, Danny would give her shoulder a gentle squeeze.

While Lily took some comfort in his presence, she knew that the night ahead would be a long one, wondering what would become of her relationship with Tony. And the days leading up to her appointment with Eric would seem even longer. She didn't know that, eleven stories below, there lurked yet another potential threat to her happiness.

* * *

On a corner sofa in the lobby she skulked, watching for Lily from behind the shroud of an *Us Weekly*. She'd considered waiting by other entrances and exits, but Lily routinely took this route, often stopping to ask at the front desk for her mail or to chat with the concierge. Always the social butterfly, she thought, then realized she had actually wrinkled her face in annoyance at the mere thought.

There had been no sign of Lily since she'd returned from the hospital that morning. Perhaps the little gift she had left at Lily's door had already done its job.

She imagined Lily collapsing to the ground with a half-eaten apple rolling off her limp palm, and it made her smile.

24
FOR WHAT IT'S WORTH

The next morning, Lily dressed her best and applied a layer of full-coverage makeup. On the drive to the hospital, she tried to calm her nerves, choosing to focus on answering emails rather than on the annoying headache that seemed to reassert itself every morning.

After responding to a message from Robert Mitchell about their lunch meeting, she checked her texts. Still no response from Tony. Not that she'd really expected one. She went back to her list of voicemails. There were several from Charles from the previous day. She had attempted to return his call, but had been unsuccessful. The last message from him had come in at four fifty-eight p.m. She hit play and listened again.

"Hey, Lil. It's me. I'm sorry I missed your call. I really do want to talk to you. But... It looks like that's not going to happen. I need to go away for a while. There are some things... things I can't really get into over the phone. Things I need to take care of before they get any worse. I hope I'll see you soon. For now, take care of yourself. Be safe." There was a long pause before he said good-bye and disconnected.

She stared at the phone as if it might give her some clue as to what was going on. She'd tried calling Charles several times since then and each time the call had gone straight to voicemail. She told herself not to be too concerned. Charles was more than capable of taking care of himself, but there was something in his voice that she'd rarely heard. Sadness. Vulnerability. She wasn't sure. Either way, it bothered her.

She didn't have much time to fret about Charles before the cab pulled up at the hospital.

Tony's father was standing outside the room when she arrived, almost as if on guard. He smiled slightly when he saw her. She wouldn't allow herself to be fooled by his typical politeness and warmth. It was still likely to be a difficult encounter.

"How is he?" she asked.

"Holding up, all things considered."

She nodded. "That's good."

They both paused and watched as a couple of nurses buzzed about behind them with a cart of supplies and what looked like a bag of platelets.

"Has he said anything to you? About what happened?" she said.

"Not much."

"Do you think I might..." She gestured toward the room.

"Um... Maggie's with him now. Why don't I go and see?"

"Thanks."

Lily waited as Joe stepped into the room. It didn't matter that the door had closed behind him. She could hear more than enough.

"Please tell her that her presence is not needed here. I'm fine. Nothing has changed. She'd do better to concentrate on the business lunch she has scheduled for today. I know how important her career is to her."

The pain and anger poured over his lips as he said the words. He didn't mention Charles. He didn't need to. The career, Hollywood, Charles—Lily knew the three were synonymous in Tony's mind at this point.

"I think *you're* pretty important to her, too," she heard Joe say.

"Dad, I know you mean well, but I'll thank you not to interfere. She made her choice. Now I've made mine. Please, ask her to go."

Joe shuffled to the door. He emerged, looking more disheartened than she might have imagined.

"I'm sorry," he said with a shake of his head.

"Don't be. I'm afraid I rather expected this."

She reached into her purse and pulled out an envelope with Tony's name on it and two small interlocking hearts drawn underneath.

"Could you give him this for me?"

"Of course," Joe said.

She lingered a moment and then nodded her thanks. She was about to walk away when Joe stopped her.

"Lily," he said, "for what it's worth, I know you love him. He loves you too. He's just in a bad place right now."

"I know," she said. "And some of what he's dealing with is my fault. I only hope I get the chance to make amends before he slips through my fingers again."

"You will," Joe assured her. "Once he's back to himself, the two of you can work this out. I know you can."

"Thank you," she said, as a tear slid down her cheek. "Thank you." She couldn't resist hugging him.

"Well," Maggie interrupted. She eased out of the door past the two of them. "I thought you'd gone."

"I ah... I was just about to go," Lily said, backing out of the embrace. "You'll... keep me posted, will you?" she said to Joe.

"I will," he agreed.

With a final nod, she turned on her heel and headed for the elevator.

"Grace called again," she heard Maggie say as she turned the corner.

25
PRIDE AND NOBILITY

Later that day, Joe slipped quietly back into Tony's room. Tony stood at the window looking out, shoulders sagging.

"Mum's gone back to the hotel for a bit," he said, falling back into the chair next to Tony's bed.

"So it's your turn to watch me," Tony said, turning from the window and coming back to sit on the bed.

Joe chuckled, pretending he didn't recognize the irritation in Tony's voice.

"You don't have to stay here, you know?" Tony said.

"I know I don't have to, but I want to. Besides, I promised you mother. And we both know what would happen if I didn't honor that, don't we?"

Tony laughed and rolled his eyes. "Well, I think your suite does have a sofa bed."

"Yes, but I'm getting far too old for that sort of thing. Best not to 'poke the bear,' as the Americans say," Joe said with a smile.

"You think I'm a fool, don't you?" Tony asked as he settled back into bed.

"I never said that. Your sister, on the other hand, has been quite vocal about it."

"Yes. I heard from her. I believe her exact words were, 'Tony, you're a fucking idiot.'"

"Ha! My Anna does not mince words."

"Does she talk that way in court, I wonder?" Tony said.

"Of course not. She saves it for you. She just doesn't want to see you make what she thinks is a huge mistake."

"Please! As if she's the queen of sound judgement?"

"She's generally quite level-headed, isn't she?"

"Dad, she told me you'd had a heart attack in order to coax me home for a bloody surprise party. Who the hell does that?"

"Okay, that particular instance notwithstanding..."

"Do you think I've made a mistake?"

"Does it matter what I think?"

Tony glanced at the letter still sitting on his table, unopened.

"I could leave you alone if you'd like a moment to read that."

Tony said nothing, but looked away.

"What do *you* think?" Joe asked.

"I think I've allowed the two of them to make a fool out of me... again. Do you have any idea what it's like to have people gossiping about the woman you love being with another man? To wonder if it's true? To question whether you're really enough for her?"

"To fear that you're not," Joe added knowingly.

"I asked her to marry me, Dad, and she couldn't even answer me." He paused, but not long enough for Joe to respond. "I can't blame her, I suppose. This Hollywood life really does suit her. And all that aside, I'm not much of a catch anymore, am I? What kind of a life could I give her?"

Joe broke in. "What did she say when you proposed?"

"Nothing. She tossed me off and ran straight to him."

"Oh, I see," Joe said. "Well, I suppose one's pride would get in the way of a reconciliation after that, wouldn't it? But she did say she had something to explain. Maybe..." He let the idea go, as Tony no longer seemed to be focused on the conversation at hand.

Tony was quiet for a few minutes before he started in again. "Charles isn't the only problem."

"Isn't he?" Joe waited.

"Something else is wrong."

"What?"

"I don't know. That's just it. She won't tell me what it is, but I know it's something. She's not well, Dad. She's had these headaches. She's lost weight. She just looks tired."

"She looked fine this morning."

"She hides it well. She's a master at putting on a brave face. You know that."

Joe nodded. Tony was right about that. As the eldest child of an angry drunk, she'd had plenty of experience at keeping up appearances. He couldn't count the number of times Tony had come home for dinner with her and her brother in tow—times when he and Maggie both knew there had been another blow up, but neither of them could get a word out of her. "Thank goodness she always had you," he said. "But now..."

"Dad, look at me. How can I possibly help her—protect her? He can. As much as it pains me to say it, at this point she's better off."

Joe shook his head. "How very noble of you."

He stood and strolled toward the window. For a while, he didn't speak. But memories of his own mistakes swirled through his head. "Tony," he said, facing him again. "No relationship is without its problems."

"I know that, but—"

"Just let me..." He held up a hand. "Things were not always so simple between your mum and me. At one time, circumstances not entirely unlike these threatened our relationship."

"When?"

"When we were young and just starting out as partners, I made the mistake of allowing someone else to come between us. I decided I wasn't right for her, that her life would be better, that she'd be happier if I let her go."

"What happened?"

"The details don't really matter anymore. What matters is that, in the end, I realized something."

Tony listened intently.

"Maggie Butler was strong and smart, hard-working, ambitious, and beguiling. And despite any faults she might have had, any bad decisions she'd made, I loved her. God, how I loved her. And dancing with her," he smiled and shook his head again. "I don't have to tell you what that's like, do I?"

Tony cracked a small, wistful smile. "Magical."

"Absolutely! Look, son, Lily is all of those things too. She is also loyal and forgiving—in some cases, to the point being self-injurious. But you can't ask her to be less than she is. From where I'm standing, she needs you. And you need her."

"Dad..."

"Pride and nobility are both wonderful qualities in small doses, but you can't allow them to stand in the way of your own happiness. I almost did. Thankfully, I came to my senses and figured out that your mother was worth fighting for. Lily is, too."

"I don't know how much fight I have in me."

"Then let *her* fight *for* you. Just don't push her away."

Joe maintained eye contact for a few seconds—long enough, he hoped, for his words to soak in. Then he turned and walked toward the door.

213

"Dad?" Tony said.

Joe looked over his shoulder. "I'm going to pop round to the lounge for a cuppa. I'll be back," he said as he stepped out.

Tony let out a long breath and picked up the envelope from Lily. He turned it over in his hand and for a second he thought he caught a hint of her sent—her lotion or perfume. His chest tightened. He turned it over again and traced the hearts with his finger before finally opening it.

26
QUELLE SURPRISE

Lily opened the door, expecting to find Danny, and instead found Tony's mother.

"What are you doing here?" Lily asked.

"I'd like to have a talk to you."

"About what? You finally got what you wanted."

"Can I come in, or are you going to make me do this from the hall?"

Lily stepped aside and motioned for her to enter.

"Thank you."

"I was just about to make a cup of tea. Would you like some?" Lily asked, channeling her inner hostess.

"Please," Maggie said. She sat on the sofa and watched Lily over the back.

"How is he?" Lily finally said as she approached with two cups on saucers she'd hijacked from the room service cart.

"That's why I'm here," Maggie said as she accepted the tea.

Lily sat facing her. "Is something wrong?" Her face immediately registered alarm.

"No," Maggie assured her. "At least, not medically anyway. Joe is with him."

"So, have you come to have it out with me for what I did to him?"

"Lily, please. You're not making this easy. I know things have been... strained between us lately."

Lily pressed her lips together, for fear of saying something rude.

"I'm sorry," Maggie said. "I don't mean for it to be that way. It just seems that ever since we arrived, every time I turn around, there *he* is again."

"He?"

"Charles," Maggie said as if she might choke on the word. "I'm sure it's only natural for one to still have some kind of connection with one's ex-husband, but—knowing the part he played in what happened before—I was... bothered."

"Is that all that bothered you, Maggie?" Lily asked.

"Is it wrong that it should bother me?"

"Of course not. But were you really worried about what Charles might do, or were you worried about what I might do with him?"

"Ah, yes. Well, there is that."

"I never cheated on Tony. You know that, right? I mean, he did tell you?"

"Yes, but for twelve years I thought you had. Forgive me, but I still have trouble removing that image from my mind. Intellectually, I know it, but as his mother, I'm

still afraid to see him get hurt. And you...
Never mind."

"No, go on. Let's just get it out there."

"All right, then," Maggie sighed. "You didn't
cheat on him. But you did cheat *with* him."

"Ah ha. There it is. Once a cheater, always
a cheater." Lily was quiet for a moment,
sipping her tea. "Did it ever occur to you," she
said, "that your son, by definition, also
cheated?"

"He wasn't the one who was married."

"True, but he certainly played a part, didn't
he? And he was a very willing participant, I
can assure you."

Maggie's mouth opened. She gave a shrug
and then cast her eyes on her tea cup.

Lily began to speak, calmly, slowly. "I was
married to Charles for ten years. I did
everything I could to make our marriage the
best that it could be, but there was always
something missing. I didn't even realize it
until Tony and I found each other again. What
we did was wrong. I won't deny that, but I
didn't intend for it to happen. Neither of us
did. And suddenly, I felt whole again... like a
piece of my soul had been restored. I love him,
Maggie. I love him more now than ever before
and I didn't even think that was possible."

Lily stopped and wiped a tear from her
cheek.

"I made a mistake. Hell, I made more than
one. But you can't understand that, can you?
Because you've never made those kinds of
mistakes, have you? You've worked all your

life to have the perfect life, the perfect family. And it *was* perfect. Until I came along."

"What are you talking about?" Maggie said, looking up at Lily.

"This isn't just about what's happening this time around, is it? It goes much deeper than all of that. I mean, Charles is a new problem. He's the cause for all of the scowls and frowns ever since you arrived, but the frequent references to Grace and her concern for Tony's well-being... Let's just get to the point, Maggie, shall we?"

"What point?"

"You never thought I was good enough for him. You still don't."

"That's not true."

"After all this time, I'm still just that fucked up little girl from the wrong side of the tracks."

"Lily..."

"That was fine when I was just your little charity case, but once we became... involved, well... that was a different story."

"You don't really believe that?"

"Don't I? From the moment we got together you were terrified that he'd end up stuck with me and all of my... *baggage*. That's what Joe called it, isn't it? You begged us not to get married."

"Stop it!"

"You prayed I wouldn't get pregnant."

"Enough!" Maggie shouted.

Lily stopped short, surprised by Maggie's tone.

Maggie took a deep breath and reached for Lily's hand. "Lily," she said, her voice stern, but motherly, "I never thought of you as just another charity case. My God. I loved you. We all did. Joe and I wanted to adopt you for Heaven's sake. We wanted to petition the courts for custody just to get you out of the Hell you were living in—to give you a real home. Even Anna was all for it. She thought it would be marvelous to have a sister the same age. But Tony," she shook her head. "He wouldn't hear of it. By the time he was sixteen he was already so in love with you, I think he couldn't bear the thought of you being his sister."

"But when we came back from France after school, he told you he wanted to marry me and you said—"

"I know what I said. I remember it very clearly, but I only wanted the two of you to wait. To be sure that was what you wanted. You were so young. I wanted you both to have time... to find your way in the world without worrying about marriage and children."

"You couldn't get me on the pill fast enough."

"Sweetheart, you were having sex at seventeen. Someone had to worry about you. You father certainly wasn't going to."

Lily bit her lip, tears glistening in her eyes. The mention of her father brought a twinge of hollow grief, but the renewed warmth in Maggie's voice filled her heart.

219

Maggie took her other hand too. "You had so much promise. You were so full of potential. I didn't want you to have to choose a baby over your career. Or worse, to choose not to have that baby." Maggie paused on the brink of saying something else. She closed her mouth slowly and swallowed hard. She blinked away tears.

Lily recognized the loss buried deep in Maggie's eyes and she suddenly understood. "I'm sorry," she said. "I never knew."

"Not many people do, darling."

"Was Joe—"

Maggie shook her head again, either unwilling or unable to go into further detail. After a minute she continued.

"I'm not proud of it, Lily. Not a day goes by that I don't regret that choice. But, God saw fit to give me two more beautiful children and I thank him every day. I've done my best to give them everything, as if it might make up for some piece of it." Maggie took another breath. "Maybe that's why I've always been so protective of them. I think that's really why I've been so cross, you know? It wasn't you it had to do with. He's my son, Lily. He's sick and he's hurting. And there's not a damn thing I can do about it."

"I hate it too," Lily said. "But you're here. That's something."

"It's not enough. And what's worse, he doesn't need me."

"Maggie, trust me. Needing your mother... that's not something one ever outgrows."

Maggie squeezed Lily's hand and smiled at her. "He needs *you*, darling."

"After what happened, I don't know."

"Do you have any idea how many times he read and re-read your text messages last night and this morning after you left? Without you, he's lost, but he won't admit it. And I don't mean just now. With you in his life, he has direction, he feels grounded. You," she paused, "You're his spot."

Lily tilted her head quizzically.

"Like in dance, you know? The spot on the wall that you keep turning back to. It keeps you steady. It keeps you from falling over."

Lily smiled at the analogy.

"Lily, trust me. He wants to reach out to you. I know he does. But he's too proud. He needs time is all. He loves you."

Lily wiped a rogue tear away. "I need him too. God... I can't lose him, Maggie," she said. "Not again." The wall of tears she'd been holding back spilled out onto her cheeks.

Maggie pulled Lily into her arms. "You won't lose him, darling," she promised. "You can find your way back. Just don't give up on him. He needs you to fight for him," she whispered as she held her.

Lily appreciated the words, but she wouldn't have needed them. The maternal embrace said everything she had been longing to hear: I'm sorry. I feel your pain. I love you.

27
THANK GOD YOU'RE HERE

She hadn't seen him in nearly forty-eight hours. He no longer returned her calls. He was clearly ignoring her. There was only one thing she could do. One person he would never ignore. Her secret weapon: Lily. Cora took a deep breath and knocked. She waited. Nothing. She knocked again.

"Just a minute," came Lily's voice.

Finally, Cora thought. "Lily, thank God you're here," she said as the door opened. She flung herself at Lily and enveloped her in a hug.

"Cora. Oh, my! What's going on, dear?" Lily asked. "Are you all right?"

Cora let go and stepped back, wringing her hands. "I don't know. I don't know what's going on."

"Come, sit." Lily said. She took a moment to throw one of Tony's sweatshirts over her tank top. "Can I get you something? Tea? Water?"

"No, thank you." Cora walked to the sofa. "Have you heard from Charles?"

"Not recently, no," Lily said as she joined her. "Has something happened?"

"I'm not sure. All I know is I haven't seen him or heard from him since Wednesday afternoon."

Lily tried to suppress the uneasy feeling in her stomach as she realized the last message she had from him came in around that same time. "Well, that's not entirely out of the ordinary for him, is it? I mean he's disappeared over night before. Out with... people," she said, choosing to ignore the fact that those were probably the nights he'd been out with other women.

"I thought that too, especially because we'd had a fight. But now it's been two nights. And he usually at least calls."

"True."

"And last night, he was supposed to have dinner with Martin Salisbury."

"You're kidding?"

"No."

Lily tried not to show it, but now she was worried, too. Not coming home was one thing, but missing a business dinner with Marty? The only thing worse would be missing a meeting with Spielberg.

"He wasn't at lunch with Mitchell yesterday either," Lily said.

"Was he supposed to be there?"

"Not that I know of, but Robert seemed to think so.

Lily took out her phone. "This is the last message I have from him," she said and played it for Cora.

Cora's hands covered her mouth as she listened. "What is he talking about? What things does he need to take care of?"

"I don't know. You said the two of you fought. Might that have had something to do with it?"

Cora looked away.

Lily tried another approach. "Do you think he was intending to stay away? I mean, did he pack a bag or anything? Take his travel documents?" she asked.

"I didn't think to look. You're right. I should've checked the safe. Why didn't I think of that? I should go, shouldn't I?" Cora said, getting to her feet. "I'll call you if I find anything." She scrambled frantically in her purse for her keys as she moved toward the door.

Lily had never seen Cora so flustered. So much for the composure of the world's most trusted assistant. She seemed almost helpless. But then, fear had a way of doing that to people. And Charles always did say she wasn't the best under extreme pressure. She checked the time on her phone. It was just after ten. There had been no word from Tony yet, even though Maggie had seemed hopeful. Lily had planned to shower and dress, to be ready in case he called, but circumstances being what they were, she decided all of that would have to wait.

"I'm going with you," Lily said. She grabbed her purse and slipped on a pair of ballet flats before heading out the door.

* * *

Lily stood in the middle of Charles's closet. Sure enough, the vintage leather duffle that he usually carried on weekend trips was missing. There was always the possibility that he'd moved things around in the year since she'd been gone, but everything else about the room looked exactly as she remembered it—right down to his favorite Armani suit left draped over the chair in the corner. Some things never change, she thought. It looked like most of his dress clothes were still hanging in the closet. At least most of the hangers were in use. She opened the drawers in the custom cabinetry. She also checked out the bathroom before leaving the master suite.

Lily heard Cora swearing as she walked into Charles's office. "What's wrong?" she asked.

Cora shook her head as she consulted the items she'd dumped on the desk. "His passport is here. His Rolex. His phone. I don't get it. Why would he leave without his phone?"

"Did you look in the box?"

Cora stepped aside as Lily rushed across the room and lifted the strongbox out of the back of the safe.

"Did you open it?" Lily asked.

Cora shook her head. "No," she said.

225

Lily frowned. "He left it open?"

"What's in it?" Cora asked.

"It's empty."

"Is that bad?"

"Not necessarily," Lily said. "But he's taken the spare phone, the cash, and the keys that he normally keeps in here."

Cora looked confused.

"The keys to the cabin," Lily clarified.

"Oh, right," Cora said. "Why the cash and phone?"

"He wanted to be able to go off the grid. He never wanted to take the chance that he could be tracked with credit cards and things. Big brother, you know? We never even used our real names."

"Do you think that's where he is?"

"Maybe. Probably." Lily took one more look in the safe and spotted two envelopes. She handed one to Cora and tore open the other.

Lily,

If you're reading this, you've probably figured out that I'm gone. I don't know how it happened, but somehow in the space of twenty-four hours my life went to hell. I wish I could tell you that I have a plan. That everything is going to be okay. But I can't. All I know is that I have to do something. I have to end it.

Everything will all come out in the press eventually. I don't think there's a way to avoid that anymore. I'm sorry for that. I never meant to hurt you.

We have had our rough moments, but when I look back on my life, my time with you has been the happiest.

I love you, Lily. I have always loved you.
Good-bye,
Charles

"What the hell?" she whispered as she finished reading. She looked at Cora, who was also wearing a concerned frown.

"It's a good-bye letter," Cora said shakily. "But he wouldn't, would he?"

Lily eyes scanned the room as she considered everything that had just happened. That's when she spotted it. On Cora's desk was a gigantic fruit basket and inside, a set of nesting dolls. "Where did you get that?" she said.

"What?"

"The fruit basket," she said. "Where did it come from?"

"Ah... I don't know," Cora said. "I thought it might be from my grandma. Her family's Russian. Someone delivered it yesterday. They weren't very careful with it, either. The card was missing and one of those dolls was cracked."

Lily didn't say anything else. On an impulse, she took off, taking the back stairs two at a time. She tore back into the master bedroom and ripped open the nightstand drawer. The second strongbox fitted inside was also ajar and empty. "Fuck!"

Cora appeared in the doorway, slightly out of breath from chasing Lily. "What is it?" she asked.

"The gun."

"What?"

"His gun. It's gone."

By the time she finished the sentence, she was pushing past Cora.

"Lily?" Cora said, sounding more frantic than before.

Lily was halfway down the stairs again. "Get the pilot on the phone."

"Where are you going?"

"Montana."

28
AN END IN SIGHT

"Forget about Lily. Forget about anyone else. Charles is the final target," she told herself as the Ferrari roared up the I-15 toward Helena at eighty miles per hour. "He is the one who has hurt you the most."

Her babushka used to say that giving gifts to the rich was like pouring water into the sea. How true, she thought. Charles had never seen her love for the gift it really was. He had taken her for granted, never noticing how valuable she could have been to him. He'd loved her, and then cast her aside like a day-old fish. Well, that was over now. She was through playing the victim. It was time he knew how it felt to be the victim.

She noted the exit number. It wouldn't be long now. Soon she would be standing in front of him and he wouldn't be able to ignore her. He would be shocked, of course. He'd always made such a big deal about keeping the cabin a secret. He thought he was outsmarting everyone, hiding the keys, having his pilot use undisclosed identities on the flight records.

But she had worked for him long enough. She had studied him and his habits. Eventually, she had come to know all of his business, all of his secrets.

She could hardly wait to see the look on his face when she walked through the door. Knowing him, he would probably be as angry as he would be surprised or scared.

She smiled inwardly as she looked down at the odometer, wondering which would piss him off more, the fact that she'd discovered his hideout, or the miles she'd put on his two-hundred-thousand-dollar sports car to get there.

29
WELCOME TO MONTANA

Just a few hours later, the jet touched down at the private airfield outside of Helena, Montana, where a car was waiting to take Lily to the ranch. The drive had never seemed so long and Lily's stomach was in knots. She tried to fill the silence by summoning more pleasant thoughts.

She thought about the cabin and all of the times she and Charles had used it as their escape. The cabin itself was quite small and rustic—just a few rooms. Most of the furniture was handmade or handed down from the owners, other than the king-sized bed with the best mattress money could buy. Charles had insisted on that. The Native American décor was never Lily's style of choice, but it seemed to work with the honey glow of the knotted pine walls. It wasn't the type of space one might expect as a retreat for a multi-millionaire, but that's what Charles had always liked about it. He always said it was like going back to his roots. A simple house with lots of outdoor space and peace and quiet to think in. Their times there had been more about the time spent together than the appearance and style of the place.

With a pang of nostalgia, Lily was jolted back to reality just in time to spot the sign for Brookside Ranch. "There," she said, indicating the entrance. She directed the driver past the large house where the ranch owners, the Hollibaughs, lived, and onto the winding road that led back to Charles's cabin on the northern edge of their property.

When they finally came to a stop, she couldn't get out fast enough. She thanked the driver as he opened her door and thrust a twenty-dollar bill into his outstretched palm as he helped her out.

"Charles," she called as she flung open the front door. "Are you here? Charles?"

No sign of him in the main room that opened into the kitchen. She checked the bedroom and the bathroom and finally rounded the corner into his tiny office. Through the French doors, she spotted him out on the large deck that overlooked the babbling brook.

"Charles!" she shouted again.

He turned and opened the door. "Lily! What are you doing here? Is everything okay?"

She ran to him, pulling him to her and hugging him. "Thank God!" she said. A moment later, she pushed him away and swatted at him. "You scared the hell out of us!"

"Us?"

"Cora and me!"

"Is everything okay?" he asked again.

"What the hell were you thinking, leaving those notes?"

He grabbed her by the shoulders. "Lil," he said more loudly "Are you and Cora okay?"

"We're fine," she said. "Why wouldn't we be?"

"Good. Where is Cora?"

"She's at home. She wanted to come with me, but I told her she should stay there in case you came back. I mean, I thought you were here, but I couldn't be sure. I tried calling your phone, but you probably didn't have a signal."

"I can't believe you're here," he said. He sounded calmer than before, but still on edge.

"I was afraid something had happened to you. You left without a word—other than some cryptic messages—packed a bag, took the cash and the gun, and took off. What the hell?" She threw her arms around him again.

"Hey," he said soothingly, "I'm sorry if I scared you. I didn't mean to. I just needed to get away. That's all. Look, I'm fine. Everything is... fine." He gestured around himself. "It's beautiful out here."

"It *is* beautiful out here," she agreed. She took a cleansing breath. "Do you remember when we used to sit out here with a glass of wine and just gaze up at the stars?" She looked up at the sky and breathed in the fresh air.

"I do," he said.

Somewhere in the distance there was a rustling sound and he startled.

"Are you sure you're all right?" she asked. "You seem... jumpy."

"Fine. Everything's fine. I'm still amazed that you're here."

"Does it surprise you that much to know that I care about you?"

"I guess not. Though you probably shouldn't let Tony hear you say that."

"Hmm." She gave a rueful, short laugh. "I don't know that he cares at the moment."

"Why not?"

"With everything that's happened, I think he's just..." she hesitated, not wanting to call him insecure. "He's not himself," she said. "And the pictures of us didn't help anything, either."

Again, something crackled down below and his eyes darted about.

Lily looked out over the railing. A doe stood in the brush on the other side of the creek, keeping watch as her baby drank. "Oh my gosh!" she said.

"What is it?" Charles said, sounding worried.

"Deer," Lily said. "What's going on with you?" she asked.

"Nothing. I'm fine. What were you saying about the pictures?"

"There's a reason you work behind the cameras, you know?"

"Yeah. Because I'm not as photogenic as you are."

"No. Because you're a terrible actor. What is it you're not telling me?"

He looked around and took a deep breath. "Okay. Sit," he said.

She sat on one of the hand-carved wooden chairs. He dragged another one of them closer and sat facing her.

"Do you remember I had some trouble a while back with a woman named Katya?"

"Your housekeeper? The one who was stalking you?"

"Yes."

He rubbed his palms on his jeans, staring at her impatiently.

"Go on."

"Okay. So, after the last incident, she was institutionalized. You knew that, right?"

She nodded.

"She managed to break out a couple of weeks ago."

"Have they found her?"

"No."

He stood and entered the office. He took and envelope from the desk drawer and brought it to her.

"She sent me this," he said. He pulled a photo and a note out of the envelope and passed them to her.

She read it.

I haven't forgotten what you did, Charlie.

"What is she talking about? Is that supposed to be a threat?" Lily asked.

"Look at the picture."

"Oh my God!" she said, horrified at the image of Charles with a target drawn over his heart. "Did you call the police?"

"Not yet."

"Why not?"

"I needed to get out of there! I thought if I came up here I could buy some time, you know, to clear my head and prepare for the media onslaught."

"Well, that is bound to happen," Lily said. "But—"

"You have no idea! And when it does... it won't be pretty. I need some time to figure out how to spin it."

Lily's eyes narrowed. "Why does it matter how you spin it? You're the victim here."

"It just does, okay? I don't want to get into it. In the meantime, Diane is keeping an eye on the situation. She's already filed paperwork for a new restraining order."

"She's got a tough job being your spokesperson, doesn't she?" Lily said, though she was well aware that Diane had, at some point, been much more than just his agent and spokesperson. "I still think you should call the police," she added.

"This is my problem, Lillian," he said, clearly frustrated. "Just let me deal with it in my way. Please." He stood abruptly and walked to the edge of the deck.

"Hey..." She followed him.

He turned toward her and she put a hand on his cheek.

"Can I help it if I'm afraid for you? I love you," she said.

The sound of those words on her lips thrilled him more than he'd imagined they would. He smiled as his fingers curled around the back of her neck.

Lily was caught off guard by the suddenly lustful look in his eyes. She opened her mouth, but before she could speak again, Charles swooped in and pressed his lips to hers. "Charles, no," she managed, but he continued his advance, forcing her mouth open wider with his tongue, until she was forced to push him away.

He reached out to her. "Lillian…"

"No," she said again, putting her hands firmly on his shoulders to keep him at arm's length.

"I want you, Lillian."

"What about Cora?"

"Cora and I… It's different. You… you're the one I need," he said. "I should never have let you go. I thought that if you had time, you'd figure out what a great team we make."

"Stop. Charles, please, just stop. I can't go down this road with you."

"We made it work once. We can do it again," he said. He pulled her into an embrace.

She shook her head. "No, we can't."

"But you love me. You just said so," he said, daring her to deny it.

"I do love you," she said. "A part of me always will, but… the love I feel for you… it's

237

not the same as what I feel for Tony. It never was," she said sadly.

His arms fell away from her as the reality of her harsh words set in. He was quiet for a minute, staring at the ground while disappointment and anger wrestled inside of him. Eventually, the pain won out and it was all he could do to contain it.

"I should go," Lily whispered, turning away slowly.

"You don't have to."

She paused in the doorway. "Perhaps it's best if we don't have anything to do with each other for a while."

Charles dashed into the cabin after her. "Lillian, it doesn't have to be like this," he said, sounding more desperate than she'd ever heard him.

She thought of Tony then and shook her head. "I'm afraid it does." She took a several heavy steps toward the door.

"Wait," he cried. "Just do me one favor," he said, rushing to take hold of her shoulders.

"What's that?"

"When all of this comes out in the news, when you hear the whole story, take a step back and remind yourself of one thing. I loved you. Okay? I love you more than I've loved anyone in a very, very long time. Maybe ever."

"Charles..."

He waved away her thought. "Don't. You don't have to say anything. Just remember what I said."

She nodded, wondering what the whole story might be. "Will you be all right?" she asked, still hesitant to leave him alone.

He shrugged. "I'll be fine here. Besides, I survived a bullet once before, remember?" He tried to sound convincing.

Lily smiled, not sure if surviving a crazy woman with a vendetta was the same thing as taking a mugger's bullet.

"I don't think you'll have any trouble with Katya," he added, knowing that he'd already asked Diane to arrange security for Lily and Cora. Still, it was only fair to warn her. "But if she should try to contact you, don't hesitate to call the cops, understand?"

Lily's forehead creased.

Charles didn't like the look. "What's the matter?"

"What if she already has contacted us?" Lily said.

"What do you mean?"

"I got this basket with a set of those Russian dolls in them. The wooden ones. I thought it was nothing at first, but then when I was at the house, Cora had some too."

"Cora? Are you sure they were sent to her and not to me?"

"I assumed so. They were painted like Michigan State football players. That's where Cora went to school, isn't it?"

"Yes."

"And now I'm thinking it isn't any coincidence that both sets had a broken doll in the middle."

239

"Shit," Charles said.

"But why would she want to..."

"Because she's a fucking nut job, Lily." He picked up his phone and cursed again. "No signal. Do you have one?"

"No."

"We need to go up to the main house and call the police."

He'd barely gotten the words out when they heard the roar of a V-8 engine gunning in the distance. He leaned over and looked out the front window to see his cherry-red Ferrari crawling up the gravel drive.

"Holy shit!" He dashed back into the office.

"What the hell?" Lily said following him.

Charles opened the desk drawer. "Fuck!"

"What?" Lily shouted.

"The gun! I don't have it!"

"What do you mean, you don't have it?"

"I don't have it!" he said again.

"If you don't have the gun, then who does?"

He looked up at the silhouette in the open doorway. "She does."

30
UNBELIEVABLE

"Why didn't you tell me you had company, Charlie? I would have brought a cake," Katya said with a smug chuckle. The words rolled off her tongue in a thick Russian accent.

"Lily was just leaving," Charles said. He gave Lily a stern look and nudged her toward the door.

"Really?" Katya said.

Lily nodded and eyed the open door. Afraid as she was to leave him, she knew she had to get out of there so she could call the police. She took a breath and stepped forward.

"I don't think so." Katya said, shoving Lily back toward Charles and kicking the door closed. "You really think I'm *crazy*, don't you, Charlie? You think I'm going to let her walk out of here? Ha! Not a chance."

She tossed her bag down on the sofa and walked toward the two of them, waving the gun around.

Charles instinctively grabbed for Lily, shielding her as best he could with his body. "How the hell did you get my gun?" he asked.

"Never mind that," Katya said. She walked in a contemplative circle around the pair. "The question is... what I'm going to do with it? Hmm? What I'm going to do with *you*? Put you out of your misery? Or let you suffer first?"

"Katya," Charles said softly, taking a new angle. He took a step toward her and tried to take her in his arms.

She stepped into him and tucked the gun up under his chin. "Don't try to sweet talk me, Charlie. It's too late for that. Over there, both of you," she said, flicking the gun toward table and chairs in the corner.

She took a bundle of rope from her bag and held the gun on Lily, forcing her to bind Charles's hands behind his back. When Lily was finished, Katya tested to the knots to be sure they met with her standards. "Good. Now, sit!" she demanded.

Lily moved toward the chair as directed, but knew there would be no hope of escape once she let Katya tie her up. She eyed Charles, who shook his head, but her mind was made up.

"Sit!" Katya shouted again.

"Okay!" Lily said, putting her hands up in surrender. She took three steps toward the chair, and in one fluid motion, grasped the back of the chair with her hand, placed one knee on the seat and extended her other leg out and around, managing to kick the other woman in the face.

"Fuck!" Charles said.

Katya stumbled backward, but unfortunately did not fall or lose the gun as Lily had hoped.

"You bitch!" She screamed, coming at Lily and swinging at her with the back of her fist, the gun still in her hand.

Lily ducked and avoided the barrel of the gun, but as she stood back up, Katya threw her shoulder into her with the force of her body behind it, knocking Lily to the ground.

As Lily lay there, Katya stood over her. She cocked the gun and pointed it straight at her. "Get up!" She growled.

Lily stood and Katya backed her into the chair, the gun touching her forehead.

Lily's head and heart pounded, but she refused to let her expression show fear. Seventeen years of dealing with her father had taught her better. Bullies only preyed on the weak. She sat, but maintained eye contact with Katya the entire time.

With Lily seated, Katya bent over to look her in the eye. "You think I won't kill you? Guess again. It's not as if I haven't tried. Why do you think this bastard had me put away to begin with?" she said, motioning to Charles. "I can just as easily try again. But this time... I won't fail. Understand?"

Lily stared back, her eyes registering confusion as she tried to process what the woman had just said.

Katya walked slowly around her, trailing the barrel of the gun along Lily's jaw line. From behind, she leaned over Lily and

243

whispered in her ear, "Don't fuck with me!" Then, with one fell swoop, she picked up the piece of pottery that had decorated the center of the table and whacked Lily over the back of the head.

"Lily!" Charles cried as Lily slumped forward in the chair. Then he turned to Katya, his gaze hard and cold. "What the fuck is wrong with you? You didn't have to knock her out!"

"How else I'm gonna tie her up with a gun in my hand, idiot?" Katya spat.

Lily awoke several minutes later to find her hands and feet bound. Her eyes still closed, she breathed deeply, trying to still the panic. She considered opening her eyes, but realized she was probably better off if she appeared to be unconscious. She stifled a groan as the searing pain from Katya's blow ripped through the back of her head. She sat as still as she could with her head down and listened, opening one eye just enough to catch occasional glimpses of Charles and Katya without being noticed.

Charles shook his head. "Why couldn't you just let her go," he said. "I'm the one you want. We both know that. You've put her through enough already."

"Have I?" asked Katya, who was now tying his feet as well. "After everything she took from me, you think I should just let her go? You think I should show her mercy?"

"She never did anything to you!"

"She stole you from me. She kept you from me and the family we might have had, and still you defend her to me?"

"You and I were over. You just refused to believe that!"

She never loved you the way I did!"

"You're going back to the loony bin for this. You know that, right? They'll find you."

"Shut up!"

"You'll never get away with it."

"Are you sure?"

"I am sure. Once I remind them of everything you've done—"

"I did what I needed to do. For us. Why couldn't you ever see that?" Katya kneeled down in front of him and looked into his eyes.

Charles spat out, "You are so full of your own shit that you can't even smell it, can you?"

She stood. "That didn't bother you when came to my room to make love to me every night, did it? Hmm? Did you think I was crazy then? You think you are such a good boy, Charlie! You filed a restraining order against me! Me! The woman you said you loved! You had me put away—you and my no-good brother!"

"You needed help."

"I needed you."

"You were threatening her. What did you expect me to do?"

"We were going to have a baby!"

"The baby you let me believe you lost?" he said.

"If you had chosen me, we could have raised him together."

"Just like that? Happily ever after? Katya, you killed her unborn child, for God's sake!"

"All you had to do was ask her to leave. But you couldn't do that."

"I loved her," he said.

"You loved me," she said.

"I cared about you, yes. But that was before I realized how deluded you were!"

"Don't talk to me that way, Charlie."

"And now, you're off your meds again and out of your mind, just like after Kristoff died."

"Stop!" Katya cried.

"You came to me claiming you needed comfort..."

"He was only five years old!"

"But what you really wanted was a reconciliation."

"You could have given us a chance."

"It was one night of pity sex! And when I told you I wouldn't leave my wife, you tried to kill her! You deliberately ran her car off the road. You left her paralyzed, for God's sake," he said, his voice cracking. He shook his head in dismay.

"She got what she deserved."

"You're certifiable!"

"Enough!" she shouted, aiming the gun at him, her hands trembling with fury. "Enough! You will never understand. You will never be sorry. The only thing left to do is to make you pay. Only thing I have to decide is which one of you I'm going to kill first! Too bad the other woman isn't here, too. I could kill them both and let you watch."

"You leave Cora out of this. She's innocent in all of this. She doesn't even know you exist."

"But she knows what it's like to love you. To share your bed. Something I should have known all of these years."

"She's never shared my bed."

"Nice try, Charlie."

"She's not my lover."

"Then what is she? Hmm? Just your assistant who shares your life, your house?"

"She's not my lover," he said again.

"Then what is she?" Katya demanded.

He gave a dramatic pause. "She's my daughter."

At that, Katya was quiet, seemingly stunned, and it was in that moment of silence that the men from the Lewis and Clark County Sherriff's Department decided to make their move.

Lily's heart nearly exploded with shock and relief at the sound of the splintering door and the words: "Drop your weapon. We have you surrounded."

31
MOTHER KNOWS BEST

Maggie looked up from her copy of *Time* as Tony eyed Lily's letter on his bedside table.

"Penny for your thoughts," she said.

He shrugged.

"I take it the letter didn't change your mind?"

"It's a lovely letter," he said. "But I don't know that it really changes anything."

"Doesn't it?"

"Mum, the fact remains that she shared things with him that she couldn't share with me, didn't she? I am concerned about her health, but what good could I possibly do her if I can barely take care of myself?"

"Do you want me to answer, or do you want me to agree with you?" Maggie asked.

"Is it possible to do both?" Tony said skeptically.

Maggie put down her magazine and moved to sit on the edge of his bed. "Well, she probably should have told you about it all. I think you're right about that. But I don't think she ever meant to keep it from you."

"You're defending her?"

"Yes, I am. I think she wanted to shield you from it, but you are just as guilty of that kind of thing."

"Please, mother."

"Don't 'mother' me, Anthony. You've been trying to convince us for weeks that you're perfectly fine, when we all know that you're anything but. That's something that the two of you need to work out. As for being useless, I don't think you have to be a superhero to love someone, or to be loved." She paused and looked at him.

He was quiet, waiting for her to continue. He could see her wheels turning. "Go on," he said.

"Can I be blunt?"

"Well, we are British, but you can try," he teased.

"Okay." She gave a nod and a cautious smile. "I won't tell you that I know what you're going through because I don't. I've never had a serious illness and neither has your father, thank God. But we are not getting any younger." She paused again. "Frankly, I don't know how much time we have left."

"Don't talk that way, Mum."

"It's true, darling. As uncertain as your future must feel, it's uncertain for all of us— even Anna and Gerald. They're perfectly happy and healthy, but for all we know, one of them could be run down by a motorbus on the way into court tomorrow and it could all be over."

"Good, Lord! I'm beginning to see where Anna gets it!"

"I'm sorry," she said. "My point is, none of us knows how long we have. The only thing I do know is that, whatever time I have, whether it's a day, or a week, or a year, there is no one I'd rather share it with than your father, no matter what the circumstances. Despite his faults and in spite of my own, we love each other and we share a history that no one else in this world could possibly share or understand."

Tony felt the lump in his throat rising as he listened to his mother's words.

Maggie watched him trying to swallow his emotion and gave him a reassuring smile before continuing.

"Your father is the love of my life," she said. "He has been by my side for more than fifty years, and no matter what happens, his is the hand I want to be holding when it's my time to go. And, if he has to go first, I should hope I'll be holding his."

As the words left her lips, Tony's eyes teared and she could practically see his heart break. Seeing him in so much pain made her own heart ache. She reached out and gently brushed his bangs out of his eyes.

"I fucked it up, didn't I mum?" he said, choking on the words.

She leaned over and kissed his forehead. "It's not too late to fix it," she said. "Call her."

He blinked several times before asking, "Could you give me a minute?"

"Of course."

As Maggie rose to leave, Tony picked up his phone, but before he could press the send button, Joe came bursting through the door with a disturbed look on his face.

"What's going on, Dad?" Tony asked.

"Switch on the telly," Joe said. "Lily's on the news."

32
FOR LOVE OF LIES

Charles found Lily sitting alone on the deck, arms folded around herself, listening to the birds chirping and the brook gurgling along down below.

"They've taken Katya."

She nodded without looking at him.

"Thank God, the cops came when they did," he said as he sat in the chair beside her.

"How did they know to come here?" Lily said softly.

"Diane," he said. "When I didn't check in with her, she got scared."

She swallowed and nodded again.

He was distressed by her demeanor. He'd never heard her so quiet and aloof.

"Are you okay?" he asked.

"Tell me about Cora's mother," she said in a far-off voice.

There was no point in lying any more. After years of trying to shield her from the truth, she'd heard it all straight from his lips. All that was left for him to do was to answer her questions and hope he could salvage some piece of their relationship. He exhaled slowly and began.

"I was seventeen. Her mother was the daughter of the farmer down the road. Her name was Maria. She was half Italian with long dark hair and a beautiful smile—a lot like you, actually. We were young and in love. We used to talk about moving to California together after graduation. She wanted to be an actress. We had so many dreams... Then, one day we had a roll in the hay—literally—in her father's barn, and she got pregnant."

"Mmm. Let me guess. You dismissed the child to follow your own dreams."

"No. Not at all. I offered to marry her and raise the baby. Maria's father wouldn't allow it. He said it would ruin her life. He forbade us to see each other and sent her off to live with an aunt in Michigan until the baby was born. She never came back. I tried to find her after graduation. I traced her to Detroit, where she was last seen, but as it turned out, she got mixed up with the wrong crowd of people and," he paused, "she died of a drug overdose. She was only nineteen."

"I'm sorry," Lily said, moved by the raw emotion in his voice.

He nodded. "Thankfully, the baby was adopted by a couple who gave her a wonderful life. I never had any contact with her until she, that is, until Cora came looking for me."

"And you gave her the job as your assistant to keep her close to you?"

"Basically."

"Why didn't you just tell me she was your daughter?"

"You already thought I couldn't have children."

"Right. And why is that again? Oh, yes! Because the fertility doctor told us you were sterile due to a childhood illness." She glared at him then. "How do you explain that?"

"I arranged for him to tell you that because I didn't know how to tell you I'd had a vasectomy."

"What?"

"I never wanted children, Lily. Not after what happened with Maria. When Katya told me she was pregnant, I realized how dangerous my lifestyle was. I had a vasectomy so it couldn't happen again. I never thought about my wife wanting children. I never planned to get married, but you changed all of that."

"You knew all along that we'd never have a baby. All of the times that you brought me here on romantic weekends with the idea of making a baby... It was all just a game to you."

"No, it wasn't a game."

"My God, I refused chemo and radiation after the tumor was removed. I insisted on finding a doctor who would do targeted therapy because I didn't want to take the chance that I couldn't get pregnant. That's what brought us to Eric."

"And it turned out to be the right decision."

"Yes, but we didn't know that at the time. I took a big risk with alternative therapy in hopes of having a baby with you, and you knew the whole time that there wasn't a chance in hell. What kind of a man does that to his wife?" She stood and walked to the edge of the deck. She leaned on the railing, fighting tears.

"I'm sorry," he said. "I should have told you. I thought that if you knew we couldn't—" He tried to put his arms around her, but she shook him off.

"While we're on the subject of things you should have told me, let's talk about the other baby—the one I was supposed to have with Tony."

"Katya saw you and your baby as a threat," Charles said.

"You and I weren't even together at the time. Why would she want to... hurt my baby?" She could barely finish the sentence.

"She hated the fact that I was letting you live in my guest house. She wanted me to throw you out. When I told her I couldn't put a pregnant woman out on the street, she decided to take matters into her own hands."

"How did you know? I never even told you I was pregnant."

"I heard you on the phone with your doctor's office."

Lily shook her head. "It still doesn't make sense. It was Tony's baby I was carrying. Not yours."

"That didn't matter to her. She decided that if you being pregnant was what allowed you to stay, then she had to take care of the problem."

"But I had a miscarriage," she reminded him.

"You thought you had a miscarriage. She switched out your prenatal vitamins with some herbal shit. I don't know where she got it."

Lily stared at him in horror. "What are you saying?"

"The capsules she put in there... caused a natural abortion."

"No," she shook her head vigorously. "That's not even possible."

"It is. I read about it after I found out."

"I would have noticed something."

"Obviously not. God, Lil, you were so fucked up over him, I don't know how you remembered to breathe."

"No!" she cried, striking out at Charles.

He grabbed her and held her as her knees went weak.

"Why didn't you tell me?" she said, finally allowing her tears to fall.

"I'm sorry."

"Why?" she sobbed.

"I didn't know, Lily. I swear. Not until afterward."

"All that time," she gasped. "All that time I wondered if I could have done something differently. I wondered if I had done something wrong. I wondered if the outcome would have been any different if I'd gone back to New York with Tony. And now..." she stopped talking and took several breaths to stop herself from hyperventilating. "If I'd gone home, Tony and I would have had our son or daughter. Who knows how many children we would have had. Why didn't I just fight for him? Our child would be alive. Oh, God. I think I'm gonna be sick."

She pulled away from Charles and leaned over the railing, letting a mouthful of bile fall into the water below.

"Lily, you can't blame yourself," he said with a hand on her back.

She reeled back to face him, now angry. "No. I can't. Can I? But I can blame her. And you. You never said a damn thing! She killed my child and she got away with it!"

"I told you, I didn't know. Not until years later."

"When, exactly?"

"After the accident. When they picked her up she was ranting like a lunatic about everything she'd—"

"The accident! The accident that you told me was caused by a drunk driver?

"Yes."

"How did you manage to cover that one up?"

"You were in a coma for more than a week. Judge Jackson helped me expedite things and she went to Shady View. She's been there ever since."

"Why couldn't you have just told me?"

"From the beginning, I thought it would only make things worse for you. I wanted to protect you."

"Bullshit! You didn't want to protect me. You wanted to protect yourself and you know it! You selfish bastard! You didn't tell me because you were afraid I'd leave you and then who would you have to smile for your precious cameras and look pretty on your arm? That's all I ever really was to you, isn't it? Good for business. Just like your agent said."

"No. Lily, I loved you. My God, I still do." He moved toward her and tried to take her in his arms.

She pushed him away. "No! Don't touch me! Don't you dare! How can you stand there and tell me that? You never loved me. You couldn't have. People who love each other don't keep those kinds of secrets."

"I'm sorry."

"Stop saying that! The only thing you're sorry about is the fact that you got caught, you son of a bitch!"

"That's not true, Lily. I never wanted things to end like this. God, I would have done anything just to be near you."

"Even sabotage my audition so that I'd be free to work for Mitchell?"

"Even that," he admitted reluctantly.

"Did you throw in with Mitchell?"

"I offered to back him if he took you on."

"Because I couldn't get the job on my own?"

"No. But I wanted an insurance policy."

"And here I thought you were just being supportive."

"That was always part of it."

"What about Eric? Did you free up his schedule too?"

"Absolutely not. Eric Channing could never be bought. He's a good man and an even better doctor. Tony seeing him was just..."

"A happy coincidence?" she said.

"You could call it that."

"You know something?" she said. "An hour ago I thought that there was a part of me that would always love you, but after today... The man I thought I loved doesn't exist. He was nothing but a lie, and the man standing before me... I don't even know him. What's more, I don't want to."

"Don't say that. Please, Lily, you don't mean that."

"I do mean it. I don't ever want to see you again. Not personally, not professionally, not for anything ever again."

"Are you sure about that?" he asked.

"What does that mean?"

"If you cut me off professionally, you could be doing yourself more harm than me." He knew it was a risky approach, but it was a last ditch effort to hold on to her.

"Is that a threat?"

"No. Just an observation."

"If the rest of this town is so comfortable in your pocket, I don't want anything to do with them either."

Before Charles could respond, a man in uniform appeared in the doorway. "Sorry to interrupt," the man said awkwardly, "but they're ready for you, Ms. Josephson."

"She'll be right there," Charles said.

"No, it's all right. I think we're through here," Lily said. She walked shakily into the cabin with the officer following her. When she stumbled and had grab onto the back of the sofa to steady herself, Charles rushed in.

"Maybe you should sit," he said. "Let the paramedics check you out."

"I'm fine!" she snapped back. "Don't try to force concern now. It's too late for that." She picked up her bag and took one last look at him. "Good-bye, Charles," she said. She took a deep breath, pushed her shoulders back and strode toward the door.

"Lily!" Charles called out as she reached for the doorknob.

The urgency in his voice caught her off guard and she looked back at him once more, against her better judgment. He looked more pathetic than she'd ever seen him.

She shook her head sadly. Her lips parted and he waited, hoping she might speak to him one last time. Instead, she let out a small sigh and fell to the floor.

33
THE FINAL GOOD-BYE

"Tylenol is fine for the pain. Otherwise, plenty of fluids and rest and you should be just fine. You'll also want to increase your protein and iron intake, but the prescription should help with that too. Any questions?"

"No. Thank you, doctor," Lily said.

"Okay. Well, the nurse will bring your paperwork in as soon as it's ready. You can get dressed as soon as you're able. Just take it easy, all right? Don't make any sudden moves for a while." The doctor smiled as he turned for the door.

"I won't," Lily assured him, sitting up slowly. She heard the doctor excuse himself to someone on his way out and looked up to find Charles standing in front of her. She was so amazed by his audacity that at first she could only glower at him.

"I know I'm the last person you want to see right now—"

"Oh, darling, what would ever give you that idea?" The sarcasm in her voice cut through him like a razor blade.

"I just had to see for myself that you were okay."

"As if you give a damn."

"You know I do."

"I don't know any such thing."

"Did they find any reason for it? Do you have a concussion?"

She didn't respond.

"Please tell me it's not the cancer."

"I'll discuss my medical condition with my loved ones when I see them. It's no longer any of your concern," she said with chilling finality.

"Fine. You've made your point. I'll go."

"Good."

"I called Danny on the way to the hospital."

"What exactly did you tell him?"

"Nothing. Other than that you'd fainted and we were on our way here. They'd already seen it on the news. I called in a favor. He should be arriving on the studio plane in an about an hour. The pilot has been instructed to take the two of you back to L.A. The car will be waiting at the airport to take you back to the medical center."

She wanted to tell him that he needn't bother, that she didn't need or want his help, but the sooner she could get back to Tony, the better.

"I also spoke with Diane. She's handling things with the police and the press. You won't have any more trouble with Katya."

"Made a few more of your 'arrangements,' have you?"

"No. I told them the truth. Everything. She'll be going away for a long time. You'll be safe now. You and Cora will both be safe."

"Good," Lily said.

"So... I guess there's nothing left to say, is there?"

Charles studied Lily's face, hoping for some sign that she still felt something besides hatred for him, but her expression remained hard. Her eyes were cold, her lips firmly pressed together.

Lily looked at him and, for the first time in a long time, maybe since she'd known him, she thought she saw something different in his eyes. Regret. She wished that mattered now, but it didn't.

After another moment, he turned and shuffled toward the door.

"Charles," she stopped him.

For a moment, hope flickered in him.

"I don't want to do this again. Ever. You understand?" she said.

He nodded and walked out.

Lily waited until he'd closed the door and then turned onto her side and let out a sob, burying her face in the pillow.

34
MOVING ON

Lily was dressed and waiting by the time Danny arrived at the hospital. She gathered her things and took one more look out the window at the sunset.

"Are you sure you're ready?" Danny said.

Truthfully, she wasn't sure if she was really ready. Walking out of that room and stepping onto that jet would mean turning her back on a huge part of her life. The idea frightened her, but she knew it was time. She had to put all of it behind her and start over. The future was full of uncertainties. There was no telling what would become of her personally or professionally. But one thing was for certain. Life as she knew it was over. Charles would always be a part of her past. But that's all he would be. The past. She had to move forward, to start fresh and face the unknown. She had to try to get through to Tony. He was her future.

"Lil?" Danny said to get her attention.

Lily nodded. She looked around the room one more time, and grabbed her half-full bottle of water from the bedside table.

"Come on, then," Danny said. He put his arm around her and ushered her out the door. "The sooner we get out of here, the sooner you can get back to L.A. and to Tony."

"Is he really all right?" Lily said.

"You spoke to him. He told you he was, didn't he? He's worried sick about you, though. We all were. Are you sure you're okay?"

"I am," Lily said, smiling and nodding. "It's been a rough couple of days, but I'm gonna be okay. In fact, I'm gonna be better than okay."

35
NEVER AGAIN

Two days ago Tony had been so hurt that he was ready to end it all with Lily, but after the events of that afternoon, none of that mattered any more. All he could think of since watching the news—knowing she'd been held at gunpoint, watching her being put into the ambulance on a stretcher—was holding her in his arms again. He paced anxiously between his hospital bed and the small window, praying for her safe return.

"You're going to wear a path there," Joe joked as Tony stopped at the window for the fourth time.

Tony only stared out at the darkness.

"You're going to wear yourself out, too," Maggie said, joining him at the window. "It's late, darling. Why don't you try and lie down for a bit?"

"I don't want to lie down, Mum. I can't rest until I know she's safe."

"Tony, she's fine," Joe said. "She told you so herself."

"Dad, she was tied up, held hostage, and ended up in hospital. I'm not going to believe that she's fine until I've seen it with my own eyes."

"And you always said your sister was the overdramatic one," Joe said.

"Touché," Tony said. He shot his father a tiny grin and turned back toward the window.

"She'll be here soon," Maggie said, rubbing gentle circles on his back.

"I hope I'm not interrupting."

Tony turned around to see Lily standing in the doorway. "Lily!"

"Thank God!" Maggie said.

Tony couldn't move fast enough to get to her. He wrapped her in his arms and squeezed her so tightly that he practically lifted her off the ground.

"Oh, my! Darling, please be careful. Don't hurt yourself."

"I'm fine. I'm fine." He backed up and sat down on the bed still holding on to her hands as she stood in front of him.

"Are you really?" she said.

"Now that you're here I am. You are a sight for sore eyes."

She looked down and caught a glimpse of herself and it made her laugh. "I am a sight all right," she said.

He examined her. She was wearing a pair of leggings and his football sweatshirt, which was almost big enough to be a dress on her. Her hair was wound up in a clip and she had next to no makeup on, but it made no difference. "I don't care what you have on. You are the most beautiful thing I have ever seen."

"Thank you," she said softly. She looked around the room at Maggie and Joe.

Joe took the hint and stood to leave, but Maggie was rooted to the windowsill.

"Margaret," Joe said, "Why don't we go round to the cafeteria and give them a bit of privacy, hmm?"

"Oh, right! Do either of you need anything?" Maggie asked. Then she caught Tony's eye. "No, of course you don't!"

"I have everything I need right here," Tony said, without taking his eyes off of Lily.

"Come along, darling," Joe called from the hallway.

Lily watched them leave and then turned back to Tony.

"How are you really?" she asked. "Are you really okay? No more episodes?"

"Yes, I'm fine and no, no more episodes."

"What about your blood pressure?"

"The doctors say everything is working as well as can be expected at the moment," he assured her.

"Thank God!"

"Enough about me. What happened to you? Tell me. I want to know everything." He pulled her closer. "But first, I want to do this," he said, taking her face in his hands and kissing her until she moaned softly.

She studied him for a moment as she stepped back, recovered her breath, and then asked, "Does that mean we're okay?"

"We are if you'll forgive me."

"There's nothing to forgive," she said.

"Lily, I was an idiot to break things off the way I did."

"You were angry and you had every right to be."

"I just felt so helpless and useless. I didn't know what else to do. I've never felt like that before."

"And I only made it worse," she said. "I'm so sorry, darling. I should never have gone to him. I should have told you everything. It wasn't him I needed, Tony. I needed you. You're my spot."

He smiled, realizing he'd heard that metaphor before. "You've been talking to my mother," he said.

"I have," she laughed.

"I'm sorry I pushed you away, angel," he said. "The truth is I need you too. I can't fight this fight alone. And as much as I hate putting you through it, there is no one on earth I would rather have by my side. No matter what happens."

A tear fell as her emotions got the better of her again.

He continued. "I know I'm not the man I was. I may never be that man again. But I want to be there for you. I want us to be there for each other, no matter how rough things get."

"I want that too," she said, caressing his cheek.

He pulled her in again, his hands on her waist. "Sit," he said.

She sat carefully on his knee and snuggled into him.

"What we need is a pact, that, whatever happens, we're going to help each other through it, okay? No more sheltering each other or keeping each other in the dark. Promise?"

She shook her head. "Never again. I promise."

"Good. Now, what do I need to know about your health?"

A nervous smile crossed her lips.

"Don't hold back, now. I can handle it. What did the doctor say about your episode?"

"It was nothing, really. Just a fainting spell."

"Did they say what caused it?"

"Fatigue, partly. That, and I need more fluids and protein, which is par for the course for me anyway and—"

"You see? I was afraid of that. You've spent so much time tending to me that you've forgotten to take care of yourself."

"No. Stop. That's not it."

"So you say."

"Yes, I do say. It's something else, but it does explain all of the symptoms."

Tony looked suddenly serious. "Was Channing right? Is it another tumor?"

Lily took his hand, placed it on her middle, and leaned over to whisper something into his ear.

He looked at her, stunned. "You're what?"

She nodded, beaming, and said it out loud. "I'm pregnant!"

"How?"

"Darling, as often as we made love, I should think you'd be aware of how it happens."

"I do know *how* it happens, but how did it happen to *you*? I thought the doctor said that it was too late."

"Well, they don't call them change-of-life babies for nothing," she grinned.

"Are you sure?"

"Quite sure."

His eyes sparkled. "I don't believe it!"

"Neither did I, but it's true."

She barely got the words out before he was kissing her again.

"I take it you're happy about the news?" she asked.

"Of course I am. Lily, happy doesn't even begin to describe what I feel right now."

"Good. Since I now have you in a good mood, I have a request."

"Anything. Name it."

"Marry me."

EPILOGUE

Matthew House, Wimbledon, England, one month later...

It was an unusually warm, unusually sunny April day and the house was quite literally buzzing with excitement as everyone prepared for the big event. The huge, three-story, white marble foyer was lined with chairs and adorned with daffodils and narcissus. A grand piano and live musicians had been brought in. No expense had been spared.

Lily was still holed up in one of the extra bedrooms on the second floor, refusing to let Tony see her. Her friend Christine had come over from Paris and she, Anna, and Lily's former assistant, Nina, were down the hall, putting the finishing touches on their makeup and donning their pale yellow chiffon dresses. Maggie fussed over Lily to be sure that everything was just perfect. Danny scurried between the two rooms, coordinating the scene.

"Lily, darling," he announced, bursting through the door with all the subtlety of Liberace, "the girls are ready when you are!"

"Almost finished," Maggie said as she fussed with a strand of hair that had escaped the twist in Lily's hair.

"Oh, God!" Lily cried out. "Excuse me," she said, springing out of her chair at the makeup table and sprinting for the en suite.

Her bridesmaids piled into the room minutes later, just in time to see Lily emerging from the bathroom, looking slightly peaked.

"Oh, no!" Nina said. "Are you okay?"

"You're not nervous, are you?" Anna asked.

"She's fine!" Danny snapped. He and Lily exchanged a knowing look. "She always throws up before any kind of appearance. Too much adrenaline. Give her some space," he added, shooing the girls with his hands to clear a path back to the vanity.

Maggie looked concerned. Lily was a consummate performer. She'd always known her to be quite calm under pressure. "You're not having second thoughts, are you, dear?" she asked as she fixed the last pin in Lily's hair.

"No!" Lily said immediately.

"I mean, with everything that's happened, are you sure you want to get married again so soon?" Maggie said.

Lily examined herself in the mirror and smacked her lips together, making sure her fresh coat of shimmering rose lipstick was coating them thoroughly. Then she turned to face Maggie. "Maggie, I have never been so sure of anything in my life."

Maggie smiled and nodded. "All right, then. What are we waiting for? Let's have a wedding!"

Thanks to Maggie's meticulous planning, the ceremony went off without a hitch and an hour later Lily and Tony were pronounced man and wife. As the guests mingled at the reception enjoying champagne and canapés, Lily slipped out the French doors that led to the back garden.

Tony noticed her exit and followed her. He stopped short at the door. There she was, leaning over the balcony in the soft glow of the sunset, a vision in her flowing, white Alfred Angelo gown. "Hello, angel," he said, stepping out.

"Oh, hello darling," she answered. "I just came out for a breath of fresh air and it was so lovely out here, I couldn't bring myself to go back in yet."

She gazed out at the garden and sighed happily. "I still can't believe we're finally going to live here."

"Believe it," Tony said. "We're home."

"It's so beautiful!"

"You... are beautiful, Mrs. Ward," he said, taking her in his arms and kissing her.

"Mmm. And you... are terribly handsome, Mr. Ward." She kissed him back, then pulled away and looked at him.

"What?"

"You look tired. Are you feeling all right?"

"I'm fine, angel. I am a little tired, but nothing I can't handle."

"Are you sure?"

"Lily, my love, stop worrying. The doctor said it was nothing short of a miracle that the kidney recovered its function again. Let's just be thankful for it and not go looking for trouble, okay?" he said, pulling her to him again. "I've never been happier than I am right now."

"Neither have I." She smiled and turned away to look out at the garden again.

"So what's wrong, then?"

"What do you mean?"

"Something's bothering you. "Are *you* feeling all right? Is it the b—?"

"Shh!" she stopped him from saying the word. "Now who's worrying?" she teased. "I'm fine. It's not that."

"What, then?"

"Nothing, really. It's silly."

"Come on." He wrapped his arms around her from behind. "Let me guess. "You're upset because Miranda and Sophie didn't have time to polish the silver and you found spots?"

"Ha ha! No. The party is perfect."

"Maybe you're afraid that the ruching on this gorgeous gown isn't enough to hide our little secret." He slid a hand down and gently rubbed her tummy as he said it.

"Isn't it? Can you tell?"

"I can tell. But then, I know it's there. And I *know* your body," he said seductively.

"Hmm. Better than anyone else in the world," she agreed.

"Oh, no! That's it!" he said.

"What is?"

"You're worried that your husband won't really be able to give you a proper wedding night!"

"Oh! Now you're projecting, darling!" she said. "I'm not worried about that at all."

"No?"

"No. And you shouldn't be, either. I know this has been a long day for you already. By the time it's over we'll both be exhausted. And anyway, I'm already pregnant, so there's no need," she teased.

"What? There is still need. I assure you!"

"Ha! Oh—"

He flipped her around to face him and gave her another intense kiss.

"Well, maybe there is... *some* need," she admitted breathlessly. "But I'm sure we'll figure something out." She touched his cheek, admiring the twinkle in his eye and the laugh lines around his mouth when he smiled. She really hadn't seen him look so happy in quite some time.

"So, tell me," he urged again.

"I don't know! I just feel like..."

"Like what?"

"Like I'm waiting for the other shoe to drop, that's all."

"Lily!"

"I know. I have no reason to feel like that. I just can't help feeling it."

"Where's my optimist, hmm?"

"Charles scared her away, I think."

"Let's not bring him into it again. Not today."

"You're right. I'm sorry," she laughed uncomfortably. "You're absolutely right. He's out of our lives, forever. We shall never speak of him again. Like Voldemort," she laughed.

"You won't get any argument from me there," Tony chuckled. "None of that matters now anyway, does it? I mean, after everything we've been through, here we are, married, happy, expecting."

"Right," Lily said, but there was still a twinge of doubt in her voice.

Tony took her in his arms and pulled her close. "What can I say to convince you that everything is going to be just fine?" he asked.

"You don't have any deep dark secrets you're hiding from me, do you?" she chided him, trying to make light.

He was quiet for a moment—pensive. Finally, he sighed and said, "Just one."

"What is that?" she asked, concerned.

He leaned in and whispered, "I was always in love with you, Lily."

"That's no secret," she said with a playful swat.

"Isn't it?"

"No."

"Not even if I told you that I've been in love with you since the day I met you? All the time we spent apart, every moment of every day."

"Really? All that time?"

"Always. And I always will be. What do you have to say to that?"

"I'd say that's good."

"Hmm." He kissed her neck.

"Very good."

"Really?"

"Uh huh. Because it just so happens that I'm arse over tits in love with you too!" she said, throwing her head back with effervescent laughter.

He laughed, too, as he held her, relishing that joyous sound.

Danny and his husband Steven stood just inside the French doors, drinks in hand.

"They really are fabulous together, aren't they?" Steven said.

"That they are," Danny said, smiling in their direction.

"Here's to happy endings," Steven said.

"Finally!" Danny added. "Cheers!"

As they stood with their glasses raised, Tony's housekeeper Miranda came rushing into the room.

"Just a minute. Where are you off to?" Danny said, stopping her as she tried to pass.

"Ms. Joseph... I mean, Mrs. Ward's phone." She held it up.

"Miranda, darling, I thought we agreed. No interruptions," Danny said.

"Yes, sir," Miranda said sheepishly. "But someone's rung five times in the last hour.

"Here." He held out his hand. "I'll take it."

"Very good, sir." She put it in his palm with a nod and rushed off again.

Danny looked at the lock screen display, then out at Lily and Tony. Without a word he slipped the phone into his pocket.

"Aren't you going to give it to her?" Steven asked.

"No."

"If they've called that many times, it could be important."

"It's their wedding day. What could possibly be so important that it can't wait until tomorrow?"

ABOUT THE AUTHOR

A native Ohioan, Cathryn K. Thompson is a teacher by day, a novelist by night, and a proud wife and mother who has always had a passion for drama and the arts. She is a lover of languages, a Toastmaster, and a former dance instructor with a brown belt in Kenpo Karate.

www.catkthompson.com